ENKI

ALSO BY V. R. R. RICHARDS

———

ENKI: Lord of Earth, Book 1
ENKI: Queen of Vengeance, Book 2

ENKI

Queen of Vengeance

V. R. R. RICHARDS

ISBN: 1535123427
ISBN 13: 9781535123426
Library of Congress Control Number: 2016911372
CreateSpace Independent Publishing Platform
North Charleston, South Carolina

To Ginny
My beautiful warrior princess.

CONTENTS

Tell me not, in mournful numbers,
Life is but an empty dream!
For the soul is dead that slumbers,
And things are not what they seem.

H. W. Longfellow

PROLOGUE

This is the story of the most desirable woman who ever lived on Earth. In Mesopotamia, in the land of Sumer, she was known forever as *Inanna*. Her name meant "Anu's Beloved." In Babylonia, she had the title of *Ishtar*, the "Whore of Babylon," because she invented the concept of sexual freedom. During century-long dynasties, the Egyptians knew her as *Isis*, the Hebrews called her *Ashtoreth*, while the Greeks and ancient Philistines named her *Astarte*. Troy honored her as *Aphrodite*, the mother-protector of her heroic son Aeneas. The people of long-forgotten Carthage continued to worship her as Ishtar, regarding her as the "Queen of Heaven," but that was before Carthage was conquered by Rome. After three bloody Punic wars, and the inexorable rise of Roman power, Inanna became overshadowed by the great pantheon of Roman gods. For centuries, she was known to them only as the goddess *Venus.*

Legends of this infamous queen still live, coming to us down through the ages as myths. So many stories from so many cultures tend to boggle the mind, distort the memory, and garble what truths may have existed earlier and now are forever lost. Perhaps the only real vision of her life was once written on ancient clay tablets, long forgotten, and only recently recovered from the ancient desert lands of Mesopotamia. This tale will attempt to clarify her royal childhood, why she left her life on a distant planet called Arra, and what extraordinary events happened to her after she arrived on Earth.

Who was she, in truth? A selfish child of royalty? A ruthless shrew, hell-bent on using any means to acquire power? Perhaps the first woman to use sexuality to manipulate men? Considering her development, was Inanna just a sudden stranger to Earth, an innocent child propelled across the cosmos to a strange land where she was victimized by a warring family, relegated to anonymity by their arbitrary rules, and unable to claim the rightful power that would have been hers on her home planet? She may have been all these identities, and more.

Some say that Inanna drove the politics of ancient Earth. Others say that her hatred of Marduk set up the final war between the armies of Enlil and Enki, the destruction of Atlantis, and the inevitable twilight of the gods. Was she saint or sinner? Madonna or whore? A wise person once said that the power of the play is that truth, whatever it is, rests in the eye of the beholder. Judge her if you will, but decide after you hear the whole story.

Chapter 1
THREADS OF DISCORD

Long ago, before the history of Earth began, King Anu ruled over a distant planet called Arra. The Arrans were robust Nordic-type humanoids, with blue eyes and golden hair. The people of Arra coexisted with a militaristic civilization, the rival planet Arkonia. In a parallel universe, far from Earth, both planets occupied a territory on the distant side of a huge wormhole called "The Black Sun." Although many had observed whole spaceships disappear into the treacherous wormhole, no one knew what happened to them. Who could possibly survive such an imaginably fatal journey? But you will learn of that event later.

King Anu was a vigorous humanoid. He had the appearance of a man about fifty-five, with crystal-clear gray eyes and thick silver-white hair. When he was very young, Anu fell in love with a beautiful Arran priestess. Id was a beautiful woman, tall and lean, with deep blue eyes and shining silver-blonde hair that cascaded down against the

1

soft white robes worn by a priestess. On her forehead was a tattoo representing the Triple Flame, three lines that flared upward and outward from the bridge of her nose to her brow. Sadly, the whole affair seemed tragic. Id was forbidden to marry Anu, because she was to become the High Priestess of Arra. On the other hand, no rules prevented her from having his child, if that was her choice. As a priestess, she had total autonomy over her own choice of a mate. So when Id conceived Anu's son, knowing he would use all his imperial power to bring about their marriage, she kept silent about the child.

Anu's duty as king was to protect Arra, and to provide an heir to the throne, so when his emissaries pursued an alliance between Arra and their neighboring planet, Arkonia, the treaty was sealed by marriage. As part of the treaty, and despite Anu's great love for Id, the king did what a king must do. Before Anu learned that Id had conceived his son, he was hurried into an arranged marriage with an Arkonian princess, a woman he had never met. This strange woman became his queen, and their son, Morgoth, became heir to the Arran throne. Or so they thought. When the Prime Councilors of Arra learned that Anu had a firstborn son by Id, the laws of Arra had to be changed. Anu's firstborn son, Eä, the true Crown Prince by Arra's old laws, could never be allowed to rule Arra.

And so the Fates, the three immortals who weave the intricate tapestry for all living things, began to spin the black threads of discord into Anu's destiny. These immortals were the *Moirai*, goddesses who personify the inescapable destinies of gods and man. The first is *Klotho*, who spins the thread that is one's life. The second is *Lakhesis*, who measures the allotments and sets the length of life. The third is *Atropos*, the one who cannot be turned. She determines when to cut the thread, thus ending life.

At birth, the Moirai would spin the thread of a future life, and then follow the steps through each lifetime. They directed the consequences of each action according to the counsel of the immortal Aeons. However, fate was mutable. The Aeons had the power to save even those already on the point of being seized from life by the fatal cut from Atropos. Imagine how busy they must have been as they assigned every life a share in the great scheme of things. But the task was not boring. Some say they were amused by their work, perhaps even laughing.

———

Inanna was beautiful even as a child. She was not only beautiful, but also clever and intelligent. Early on, she had the ability of astute observation, a talent often used to manipulate those around her. Although she was born into the rosy world of Arra, with all the abundant advantages and pleasures of a royal princess, she knew little of what went on beyond the palace garden where she played with her twin brother, Utu.

From birth, she saw herself as the center of her own universe, a place where everything revolved around her. Whatever she wanted, she need only command a retinue of those ready and willing to fulfill any and all of her childish wishes. Growing up in this pampered environment, she soon became aware of the value of power. She learned about it by observing the significant men in her life who wielded it: Anu the king, Morgoth her father, and her nasty half-brother Ninurta, Morgoth's eldest son.

She watched these men from afar. She knew little of her father, except that he was the Crown Prince and would one day rule Arra. From the stories her mother told her, she learned that Morgoth had been sent to Arkonia when he was a young boy. His experiences at military school hardened him, especially at the hands of the cruel Arkonian boys who taunted him for being half-Arran. Although he had become a decorated officer by the time he returned to Arra, he had lost any semblance of Arran compassion, or the ability to love.

Inanna knew nothing of Arkonia, only that it was a strange world that shared the galaxy with Arra. She found no interest in politics or intrigue. Treaties were boring, and she didn't understand the sinister rumors or the mysterious activities surrounding Anu's Arkonian Queen. Formerly called Sh'Ka on her home planet, Queen Antu was a thin reptilian humanoid in her early fifties, with yellowish eyes and a greenish caste to her finely scaled skin.

Inanna never really knew Antu or spent any time with her, even though she knew the strange alien was her grandmother. The Queen was a mystery to her, a frightening image to be avoided at all costs. According to her mother's stories, the Queen's power came from an alien world, as did Morgoth's, but she did not want to think about that. That subject would not ever concern her.

The palace on Arra was small and safe, and the young Inanna believed it would serve all her needs until Fate ended her life. Here she was surrounded by comfort and wealth. She was a child that would always be catered to by others, as if they wanted to absorb her beauty and her power. She believed that she could do almost anything, because she knew that King Anu adored her and would always intercede on her behalf. As Anu's beloved, she knew, beyond any doubt, that she was born to rule.

But then, without warning, everything changed. She remembered the day she and her brother Utu learned that their father, Morgoth, would no longer be the Crown Prince. Sneaking into the hidden balcony overlooking the Grand Council, something they had done many times before, they watched the horrible drama playing out below them. A very tall and dignified Prime Councilor, quite old, stepped forward to announce that the Grand Council had been called to an emergency session. They were to decide which of King Anu's two sons would succeed him to the throne. The two children stared at one another. What was happening?

Morgoth was Eä's half-Arkonian younger brother, about thirty-four, hardened and dark. On Arkonia, he was called Kha'Dok at military school. Now wearing an officer's uniform, Morgoth appeared Arran, except for his closely cropped dark hair, light olive skin tone, and greenish reptilian eyes. He stood apart, coldly impersonal. In contrast, Prince Eä was handsome and vibrant, about thirty-five, with blue eyes, fair skin, and long ash-brown hair.

Morgoth knew he was the Crown Prince, so he became irate and protested in a loud voice. Apparently, the loudness of his objection didn't matter to anyone. Anu reminded him that the coveted title had been bestowed on Morgoth *before* Arkonia attacked Arra. Present necessities required serious changes. The Queen lashed back at Anu with the fury of betrayal. As a condition of their marriage, Anu had pledged that any son born to them would be heir to Anu's throne. Now she accused Anu of scheming to cast Morgoth aside. Anu explained to her that because Morgoth was half Arkonian, Arrans would never accept him as their future king in the event of war between Arra and Arkonia.

Once again, Morgoth protested. After all, if he was Anu's son the people of Arra must accept him. Unfortunately, the Prime Councilor reminded him, Morgoth was Anu's heir only by the treaty made at the time of Anu's marriage to his Arkonian queen. Under Arra's old laws, the firstborn son was the rightful heir to the throne. That would be Eä.

Then things got ugly. Antu turned on the Prime Councilor with all her wrath, and claimed that Eä's mother was merely a concubine to Anu. Since Eä's birth had been illegitimate, Eä's claim to the throne was also illegitimate. More to the point, Antu was Anu's wife by lawful bond, while Eä's mother had been Anu's *whore*.

Livid, Eä rushed to Id's defense, outraged by Antu's insult. Not only was Id his mother, but she was the High Priestess of Arra. According to Arran beliefs, the High Priestess may have a child by anyone she chooses, but she is forbidden to marry. She lives only to serve the great goddess Sophia, and the people of Arra.

To quell the animosity between Eä and the Queen, Anu immediately called for a decision. In their great wisdom, the Councilors restored the old laws. From that day forward, the firstborn son of Arran blood would be heir to the throne, above all other sons. With that proclamation, Morgoth was deposed.

One would think that Eä would be happy to have his rightful title restored, but he was not. He refused to be Crown Prince, but his loud protests were drowned out by the boisterous cheers of others. When calm returned, Eä repeated his refusal for all to hear, confirming that he had no interest in politics or power.

After an ominous silence, Anu glared at Eä, now furious. In a loud voice, Anu then offered Eä an ultimatum: "Obedience or exile!"

Before Eä could respond, Morgoth strode across the room and, with malice, struck Eä across the face with a merciless backhanded blow. Eä fell to the floor, stunned.

Morgoth stood over Eä, snarling, "You'll never be king. Never!"

Eä got to his feet, and moving forward to only inches away from Morgoth's face, he snarled back. "Idiot! I don't want to be king. Not now, not ever."

———

Confused and frightened, Inanna and Utu crept from their hiding place and ran to their mother. Sud could not believe their story. The whole family was in turmoil. Whatever expectations they had for their future were now gone. Sud tried hard to stay calm, fearing Morgoth's rage when he came home. So she gathered the children about her and did her best to explain away the violence they had witnessed between Morgoth and Eä.

Once Morgoth had been Eä's best friend, she told them. That was when he was Inanna's age, but then Anu had sent him to Arkonia, and after all those years of military training among such strange people, Morgoth had changed. He had grown cruel. Now he only did what was expedient, not what was morally right. Sud did not know what they had done to him on Arkonia, but Morgoth seemed to have lost his moral compass, as well as any compassion for others. These days, it was all about duty. Nothing else. *Now what?*

she wondered. *Without the crown, what would he do?* She did not want to think about it.

———

Red lights flash. A shrieking alarm sounds a warning.

Anu shouts, "Turn on the orbiter!"

Officers gape in terror as turbulent reddish-orange clouds slowly envelope the entire Arran planet. A huge hole opens over one pole allowing a multicolored curtain of charged particles to pour into the lower atmosphere.

"Merciful Sophia! Save us all," says a Major.

Eä strides into the room. He watches in stunned amazement with the others.

"What's happening to us?" Anu demands.

In the orange clouds, random lightning flashes with loud crackling discharges. The sky seems ready to ignite. Charged particles continue streaming through the hole in a glowing aurora of eerie light.

"A Rift!" Eä breathes, almost whispering the horror of what he sees.

Without warning, the ground rocks violently. In response, the signal from the orbiter breaks up, leaving them blind, then in the next instant becomes clear again. In greater terror now, they watch several volcanoes explode, belching molten rock and orange noxious gases.

"How could this happen?" Anu demands.

Eä frowns at him. "I warned you."

"Morgoth?"

"Who else?" Eä answers. "Only high-energy plasma caused by Morgoth's weapon could burn through our magnetic shield like that."

"Tell us what to do," Anu pleads.

"I wish I knew," Eä says, stymied for the moment. "Maybe nothing."

———

The minute Sud felt the tremors, she knew at once what Morgoth had done. She had overheard him talking about his new Arkonian weapon for months, how it would create a web around the entire planet and destroy Arra's enemies, and his fury at Anu because he would not let him use it. She was surprised when Morgoth took her into his confidence and shared his plan to test the weapon despite Anu's restraint. He reasoned that if he could show everyone on Arra how powerful his weapon was, the public would know Anu was wrong. "When the people know that I saved them," he had bragged, "Anu will have to restore my title." Daring to return to his cherished vision of ruling Arra as king, he said, "I will be Crown Prince again."

Today she heard the emergency broadcast about the Rift. Morgoth's weapon was a catastrophe. The announcer said high energy had caused a rip in the upper atmosphere. A huge hole had opened over one pole that allowed an avalanche of charged particles to pour into the lower atmosphere. Arra's natural shield was ruptured, and now it failed, tragically. Turbulent reddish-orange clouds were enveloping the entire planet, a suffocating blanket that could end all life, in time. She gasped at the reality of it. *What will we do? Where can we go?*

When Morgoth entered Sud's rooms, he was with Anu. Sudden anxiety flooded her mind. *Will Anu arrest him?* she wondered. Her brow was wrinkled with a thousand questions.

"What's going to happen to us?" she asked.

"Don't look so worried," Morgoth said to her. He threw his quirt on the table, the one he always carried with him, and removed his coat. He turned to Anu, "Eä is going to fix everything, isn't he Father?"

Anu frowned at him. "You'd better hope so," he said.

"Fix it?" Sud looked confused. "How?"

"Eä's going on an expedition." Morgoth gave a throaty snicker. "In search of gold."

"Gold," Sud said, looking cynical. "What good will that do?"

"It's complicated," Anu said, trying to remember what Eä had told him. *The Rift was caused by hot plasma that left a trail of highly charged ions.* Anu tried to explain what he remembered. "Superheated plasma sliced a hole in our upper atmosphere, like a hot knife through butter." He paused to collect his thoughts. "Eä thinks the heavier electrons in gold will bind to the highly charged ions left in the Rift. He thinks gold will act like a catalyst and neutralize the field," he pauses, and then rushes to finish, "by diffusing the charge as photons. Once discharged, the Rift should close." Anu smiles in triumph.

Sud smiles back. *Silly old fart*, she thinks.

Just then, young Inanna, stunningly beautiful at eleven, runs into the room with her twin brother chasing her. Anu's guards attempt to stop them, but Anu waves them off.

With her black curls bouncing, Inanna runs to Morgoth. Excited and out of breath, she gazes up at her father with through thick lashes framing her irresistible dark almond-shaped eyes.

"Mother says I'm a princess now. That means I'll be a queen one day, doesn't it?" she implores, as if expecting him to settle the argument.

Annoyed by the interruption, Morgoth frowns at her. Protective of the girl and charmed by her exotic beauty, as always, Anu intercedes. He takes off his crown and puts it on Inanna's head, smiling his unwavering approval.

"You shall be Inanna, Queen of Heaven," he proclaims.

She immediately throws her arms around his neck and smothers his cheeks with her kisses. "I'll be like you, Poppy, and rule all of Arra," she promises.

Anu chuckles.

Utu watches in disgust while Inanna flaunts the crown in triumph. Hoping to explode her self-important bubble, he jabs, "Girls can't rule. Only men."

Impervious to Utu's attempts to ruin her show, she ignores him. Quick as a fox, she snatches up Morgoth's quirt and wields it like a scepter. In a haughty voice, she declares, "When I am Queen, I shall rule all of heaven." She struts about the room with regal pomp, waving the quirt at her imaginary subjects.

Provoked by Inanna's snooty airs, Utu's devilish nature emerges. He sneaks up, snatches the crown from her head, and runs off with it. With the magical splendor of Anu's crown gone, Inanna chases Utu in a vengeful fury, waving the quirt and shouting, "Give it back! Give it back!"

Utu leads her around in circles, giggling, while Anu laughs at their entertainment. Impatient, Morgoth catches Utu and takes the crown from him. "Utu, that's enough," Morgoth commands. He grabs the quirt from Inanna and points to the exit, "Out, both of you."

Utu prances out, moving his hips with a queenly wiggle, a mockery of Inanna's regal performance. When he glances back at her, Inanna sticks her tongue out at him and marches away in royal grandeur, snubbing him.

Anu replaces his crown. Smiling, he says, "She's a beauty, that one."

"Yes, but you shouldn't spoil her like that," Morgoth argues. "She's already too headstrong."

Anu gives Morgoth a knowing glance, "Like her father, eh?"

———

Despite the many obstacles in his path, Eä finally left Arra to search for gold. Anu provided him with Arra's latest starship, a crew of the best astronauts, and seven forbidden weapons. When Id, the High Priestess, came to see Eä off, she gave him a complete set of the sacred codices to take with him. These were rare crystals containing all the secret knowledge of the Aeons. She also gave him a remarkable man-sized android named Bog, and last of all, she gave him her own precious amulet as a means of contacting her from almost anywhere in space.

Although Eä left his wife and younger children behind, he found it more difficult than he had anticipated. Both Marduk and Lugal begged to go with him, but Damkina forbade it, insisting that they were too young. Eä agreed that Lugal, Dumuzi, and Geshtina were too young, but he also remembered being a teenager, like Marduk. At fifteen, Marduk was impatient to learn and yearning to experience life. So Eä softened, but when he beckoned to Marduk, Lugal became furious at being left behind. Raging at his father and jealous of his brother, he shouted at them, "I hope you never come back!"

Eä remembered turning back to Lugal, seeing him standing there, so defiant, with the boy's last words echoing in his mind. He knew he could never explain to Lugal how hard it was to tear himself away from him, from his home, from the only life Eä had ever known on Arra. But Eä knew he had no choice. He'd do whatever he had to do to save Arra, and perhaps Lugal would come to understand someday.

At first, the trip into space seemed exciting, but soon the monotony of space travel wore on him. He was bored by the time they reached the center of the galaxy. But then everything changed when Bog sensed the presence of danger. Bog was the first to warn Eä, before anyone else. Eä looked but saw nothing, so Bog's warning seemed only a false alarm. When Bog tried to warn the others, Eä snapped at him, "Let those who are more experienced run the ship, Bog." Then they all saw it. A huge black hole loomed directly in their path. Already caught in its inescapable field, their ship plunged into the inky blackness, swirling around and around, plummeting like a bug down a drain.

Using his superior strength and skills, Bog took the helm and guided the struggling ship, groaning and pitching all the way, to the calmer outer edges of the vortex. Time seemed to stand still. Eventually, to everyone's astonishment, the ship spun out of the wormhole and into a magnificent parallel universe. They found themselves in a glowing milky-white galaxy filled with millions of jewel-like stars that sparkled against the midnight backdrop of space. The starship moved forward through a belt of icy objects that glistened like crystals in a magical frozen land. Slowly and carefully, they edged their way through obstacles and moved toward a bright blue-green planet wrapped in a puffy cradle of snowy white clouds. This would be Eä's new land. They called it Earth.

Below, they saw a lush green valley lying between two rivers. After landing, they climbed into the hills to explore. From a high point, Eä gazed down into the valley, admiring the beauty of this strange new world. How unlike Arra it was. Clear blue sky, not rosy. Puffy white clouds. A brilliant golden sun. Crystal blue rivers. And thousands of animals in a great green valley. He never expected to find such beauty.

Anu was relieved to hear the news that Eä had found gold. Despite the good news regarding the great quantities of gold that were present, the bad news was that he couldn't say how long it would take to mine it. So much work had to be done before the gold could actually reach Arra, and even then, would the gold really close the Rift? Too many problems remained.

Anu reminded Eä of the urgency. The Rift had been growing larger ever since Eä left. Anu painted a grim picture, and a frightening future. Arra's rosy sky was now an eternal gray, the grass was yellowed, and the once-abundant flowers had stopped blooming. Anu feared a famine. Eä assured him that he was doing his best, but Arra should be prepared for a long wait. He cautioned Anu that if Arrans begin growing ill, or dying, they would have to leave Arra.

———

By the time Marduk was seventeen, Eä had made considerable progress in establishing a frontier colony on Earth.

After four shars on Earth, no gold had yet been delivered to Arra. Part of the problem was that only the Arrans could open a portal to Earth from their universe. Finally, a huge mothership from Arra emerged through a stargate and hovered overhead. Eä gazed up at the marvelous sight, recalling his fear that he might never see a ship from Arra again. He watched a shuttlecraft descend to the Landing Place at Eridu.

A woman in her early thirties, stunning in her Chief Medical Officer's uniform, stepped off the shuttle carrying a suitcase and a large shoulder bag. She was Varda, lady of the stars. She was tall, sexy, and stacked. Eä stared at her, captivated. Behind Varda, fifty nurses from her medical staff left the shuttle.

Varda gazed at her new surroundings with a critical eye. Eä rushed to greet her, displaying his most charming smile. She stiffened, standing proud and petulant. Feeling her chill, Eä handed Bog her gear. Bog hesitated, and then led the way to her quarters. She followed the android, hurrying to keep up.

"Not very friendly, is she?" Marduk muttered.

"Don't worry," Eä said. "Ice melts."

———

The days went by quickly as Eä expanded his mining operation. He put his best officers in charge of computers and records, building living quarters, drilling the main shaft for the mine, and for himself, constructing the central power system.

"Out in the valley," he had told them, "we'll build a pyramid tuned to the same crystal harmonics as this planet. Once built, we can draw power directly from the Earth's grid."

Eä and his men rose to the challenge. Using a powerful cannon-like laser, they burned a deep vertical shaft down into the base of the mountain. From the main shaft, they dug out horizontal passages, or *stopes*. Chunks of blasted rock dropped down into to a conical machine that crushed rock into ore, and then dumped the ore onto a conveyor belt that took it to waiting carts. The ore moved along on a cushion of energy, travelled down another chute, and then into the cargo hold of a Sky Transporter.

While the mining operation proceeded in the Abzu, Eä returned to his strategic command post in Sumer. On a hill overlooking the frontier city of Eridu, Eä built a colossal ziggurat, a seven-level stepped platform that supported his royal residence at the top. Deep in the interior of the ziggurat, he constructed his control room. Along the walls were huge holographic screens monitoring strategic aspects of his entire mining operations.

To his surprise, Varda stormed in with the fury of a tornado. "We still don't have a decent clinic," she bullies. "How much longer do I have to wait?"

With a charming smile, he shows her to the computer. "Sit here," he says, attempting to soothe her temper. "Let me show you my plans." Intrigued, she complies.

He projects a raised-relief model of the seven cities that run along the two rivers dividing the valley. A red arrow, pointing northwest, runs along the Euphrates River from Eridu to Sippar.

"This red arrow is the landing path," he explains. "We're here, at Eridu. The refinery is there, at Bad-Tibira. The gold goes from there to..."

"Yes, yes. To the mothership," she interrupts, growing impatient.

He ignores her bitchy tone, and with a good-natured smile, he continues. "...to the shuttlecraft at Larak, and then to the orbiting platforms."

He moves behind her, noting the almond fragrance of her hair and the enticing curve of her hips. Standing close, and reaching over her shoulder, he points to the screen.

"Our spaceport goes here, at Sippar," he says. Your medical building will be there, in Shuruppak. I'm drawing plans for Mission Control in the central palace at Larsa. Then we'll get to your clinic."

She glares at him, ready to explode.

"But not yet," he adds, before she can start another tirade. "Once injecting the gold works on Arra, the rest will be easy."

"Untested procedures usually lead to failure," she states in an icy tone, stifling her anger.

"We're ready to run the test now," he says, smiling seductively as an antidote to her harsh pessimism. "We developed an aerosol mist to suspend the gold dust inside the clouds. Care to watch?"

———

On Arra, roiling clouds from the Rift cast an eerie gray-orange pall over the entire city of Astra. Anu's palace gardens appeared sickly, wilted, and with none of the luxuriant flowers that had once graced the grounds.

Inside the palace, Communication Center a red light was blinking nervously. Anu sat at the huge wall of screens, awaiting the missile launch. Morgoth stood near him, scowling. The countdown from Earth began.

"Five, four, three, two, one!" boomed Eä's voice over the space communicator.

The probes launched. Above the churning clouds, payloads exploded. Gold dust rained down, then spread out, suspended above the churning Rift. As the gold dust drifted down into the Rift, sprays of whirling gold dust exploded like fireworks. They all waited, but the Rift remained unchanged.

"Just as I expected," said Morgoth. "Gold won't ever..."

Anu turned to Morgoth, ablaze. "You try my patience to the limit!" Anu exploded, cutting him off. "Not only did you disobey my orders, but you caused a catastrophe that put our entire planet in danger. What you did was treason, and now you attack the only plan that might save us. I'd have you arrested and put in prison, but then we'd have no heir... and your mother would never stop nagging me."

"I wanted to protect us," Morgoth reasoned. "Do you know what would happen to Arra if another species invaded us?"

"I've heard enough of your claptrap!" said Anu. "Pack up. I'm sending you to Earth."

"Earth!" Morgoth choked back his ire. "No, my work is here."

Anu sniffs contempt. "What work?" he demanded. "The Rift? That was your work, wasn't it? So go fix it — but mind your place. You're not in command on Earth, Eä is."

"You said a Crown Prince should bow to no one."

"Well, now I'm saying you'll take orders from Eä. He'll be the Crown Prince when he returns."

"Don't you mean, if he returns?" Morgoth demanded, even more resolute and set to argue.

"Go!" Anu shouted, losing his temper. "Varda will make sure that I'm obeyed."

"Varda!" Morgoth exclaimed, glowering. His voice grew menacing. "Leave that book closed."

"If it's a problem, take your family with you," Anu replied, secretly enjoying Morgoth's wretchedness.

Morgoth growled softly. The mess with Varda flashed through his mind. *It was all her fault, wasn't it?* He hadn't meant to rape her, but she had resisted him, made him burn with passion. In that terrible moment, he had to have her. *Bloody whore.* She had reported him, sent him into exile. It was so long ago. Now he had a new life, the opposite of what he thought he had wanted before Varda. In a move to restore Anu's good will, he had married Sud and taken responsibility for Varda's son. His son. With Sud, he had raised Ninurta, made a man of him. *Why couldn't Anu leave it alone?* Varda would dig up all those old bones, and their shades would come back to haunt him. *A Gorgon's curse upon her! Would it never end?*

Anu grew commanding. "You'll all stay on Earth until Arra is safe. *All* of you. Understand?"

"On that repulsive frontier, with Eä?" Morgoth seethed, raging inwardly against his father. "Never!"

Menacing, Anu replied, "I give the orders here, not you."

Morgoth moved forward, as if ready to attack.

This time Anu's voice was ominous. "I warn you, don't take another step."

Morgoth drew back, then turned and stomped out.

Chapter 2
JOURNEY TO EARTH

Preparations for the journey to Earth had been frantic. *Everything is happening too fast*, Inanna thought. She had cried, and argued, and refused to go, but Morgoth tolerated none of it. "We'll go! And that's an end to it," he commanded. When she approached her mother for support, Sud told her, "Anu commanded us to go with your father." Utu was too excited about going on a journey into space, too excited to bother with his sister's tantrums.

As the time to leave drew closer and she grew more terrified of going to some strange planet, far from everything she knew and loved. Finally, Anu convinced her. "Don't be afraid, my pet," he told her. "I know you want to stay here, but Arra is not safe now. A new world can be an exciting experience, one filled with new possibilities. No matter what happens, you are Anu's beloved, so be strong. Remember, a queen must have courage."

Like you, Poppy, she reminded herself, feeling Anu's strength within her. Her mother was distant during the trip, and Morgoth was of little comfort since he seemed perpetually angry and sometimes volatile at the slightest disturbance. Sud had told her, "Leave your father alone. He's too upset about this trip to bother with your silliness." *What did she mean?* Inanna wondered. *Why won't anyone tell me what's happening?* At last, Utu explained to her what little he knew.

"Think about Father," Utu said to her. "Anu is holding him responsible for the Rift. How would you feel after being deposed, your crown given to someone else, and then exiled to a remote planet where you're forced to work with the same person who took your place?"

"That's mean, Utu. Anu, blame Father?" she asked. "You're making up stories again, just to tease me."

"It's true," he argued. "Father disobeyed Anu. Mother told me he fired a terrible weapon that caused the Rift. That's why she's so upset, but they don't want to worry you."

"I'm not worried," she said, sounding petulant. "I just want to know when we're going back home."

"We may never go back," Utu said, looking at her with a very serious face.

Her eyes grew wide. "Never?" she exclaimed. Her thoughts raced. *Never to see Arra again. How could that be?*

"They said our only hope would be mining enough gold to close the Rift," Utu said, trying to reassure her. "If the gold works, then we can go home. If not, we stay."

She stared at him. "Forever?"

He nodded.

She began to wail. She kicked her feet and pounded her fists on the bed, growing hysterical.

Sud came in. She took one look at Inanna and sent Utu out of their cabin. "What's wrong with you, Inanna?" she asked, with a gentle voice.

Inanna sat up, her face red and wet with tears. "I want to go home!" she moaned.

Exasperated, Sud said, "Let's not go through all that again." She poured some water on a cloth, wrung it out in a basin, and proceeded to wipe the tears from Inanna's face. "Don't you realize how lucky we are to leave Arra right now?"

Inanna shook her head.

Sud went on, "The city of Astra is covered with thick clouds from the Rift. Dust is on everything. The gardens at Anu's palace are wilting and all the beautiful flowers are dying. Unless the Rift is closed, the people will grow sick, too. If that happens, everyone will leave Arra. No one will be able to return."

Still sobbing, Inanna asks, "But if we can't go back to Arra, Mother, how will I ever be a queen?"

Sud stares at her daughter, growing impatient with her. "Really, Inanna. Is that all you ever care about?"

———

The end of a long and boring journey came at last. The starship arrived at Earth. Now the families had to wait at a space platform until they docked, and then for shuttlecrafts to transport them to the surface. As large and comfortable as the starship was, the whole trip had been stressful for everyone. With Morgoth's animosity toward Eä expressed often, Sud and Damkina tried to stay apart to avoid his wrath, but it was impossible to keep their children isolated. Although Morgoth and Ninurta preferred to eat with the ship's crew, the two wives would meet briefly when they brought their children to meals.

Damkina did not want to leave Arra any more than Sud, but Anu had insisted, so she packed up the house and along with young Geshtina, only eight, Dumuzi, thirteen, and Lugal, fifteen. Sud was relieved that Morgoth's presence kept order whenever inevitable arguments flared among the children over silly things. Sud's twins, Inanna and Utu, both thirteen, interacted with Dumuzi mostly, and sometimes with Lugal. Ninurta, now seventeen, spent time with Lugal, but mostly kept to himself. Geshtina hovered around Sud, too young for any social games or interactions with the teenagers and often feeling left out. None of the children knew what life on Earth would be like, and without words or images of any future possibilities, they talked only of Arra and the life they had left behind. Any questions about Earth only reminded them of their insecurity and left them speechless.

All that changed when the shuttlecrafts came for them. Curiosity about their new world pushed everything else out of their thoughts. Eä's wife and children were the first to land. Damkina, now a stately forty, watched while Geshtina and Dumuzi rushed to Eä and into his strong arms. Eventually he came to her and gave her a dutiful kiss on one cheek. Lugal stood by himself, scowling at Eä and Marduk.

Sud saw them as she stepped from her shuttlecraft onto the landing pad. She noted Lugal's sour expression and Damkina's cold reserve, thinking to herself, *This does not bode well for them.* She stepped aside to watch Inanna and Utu step down. Utu seemed eager and curious, but Inanna was frowning. Sud could read Inanna's displeasure at the first impression of her new surroundings. They all knew at first glance that Earth was not Arra.

Sud and the twins waited while Ninurta, as arrogant as his father, stepped down from the shuttlecraft and surveyed the surroundings. He was followed by Morgoth, now wearing full dress uniform. Morgoth glanced up at the blue sky, the white clouds, the lush green foliage, and then he spat with contempt.

Almost completely hidden by thick bushes along the landing pad, a group of white-faced natives began chattering loudly at the sight of Morgoth.

Inanna tugged at Sud. "What's wrong with them, Mother?"

"They look like they're frightened," Utu said. He gave Inanna an evil grin, "Maybe they're going to eat you."

Inanna screamed, and then tried to hide herself behind Sud.

"What's wrong with her now?" Morgoth demanded, scowling down at his daughter.

"The natives frightened her." Sud smiled at him, attempting to soften his anger.

Ninurta tapped Morgoth's arm, distracting him.

Morgoth looked up.

Varda was striding toward him from across the landing pad.

Great gorgon's guts! Morgoth thought with disgust. *She's the last person I want to see.*

———

With little housing available on the frontier, especially with luxuries expected by royalty, Morgoth and his family had little choice but to accept the generous offer to share quarters in Eä's lavish palace.

"It's only temporary," Eä had said, "until we can build more suitable housing for you."

"How soon will that be?" Morgoth demanded, impatient to be elsewhere.

Eä knew that Morgoth had brought more than three hundred Igigi to Earth. They were now housed on the space platforms in orbit above Earth. The Igigi were hardened warriors from Arkonia, gleaned from the orphans who were found living in the ghettos of Arkonia where they had learned to fight, hate, and kill at an early age.

"That depends," said Eä, reminding himself to be cautious. He would have to stay several steps ahead of Morgoth from now on. *Maybe we can use Morgoth's Arkonian scum to help build our new ziggurat at Larsa*, he thought.

"On what?" Morgoth demands, already suspicious.

"If we had more labor, we could build our ziggurat for Mission Control much faster. If you're in a hurry, you could let us use the men you brought with you."

"The Igigi? That's outrageous!" Morgoth bellows. "They're warriors, and too proud to become mere laborers."

Proud? Eä muses, thinking how ironic to call thieves, murderers, and sewer lizards "too proud" to work honestly. "Suit yourself," Eä says. "You're welcome to stay here as long as you like," he adds, knowing that was the last thing Morgoth would want.

Now it was a question of waiting, Eä knew. *Which would be worse for Morgoth*, he wondered, *living here, with me, or building Mission Control under my command?* If Morgoth could tolerate neither, maybe he would pack up and take his Igigi scum back to Arkonia, where they belonged.

Life for Morgoth in Eä's ziggurat was not pleasant. Inanna could not be consoled, and she complained constantly to everyone near her.

"I hate this place," she often wailed. "No friends, no servants. With so much to do, you expect me to work, work, work. Just look at my hands! I never have any fun anymore. No dances, no parties, no games, and no one to even care how I feel."

For the most part, Morgoth and Sud ignored her. When she complained, they told her to think of all the people on Arra who were much worse off, all of them trying to exist on a dying planet. Didn't she realize how lucky she was?

Utu did not fare so well. Being closest to her, he was the only person who had to listen to her constant complaints.

"How can we live like this?" Inanna demanded.

Utu just shrugged. *How can I know how we should live, or even if we will live? Only the Moirai know that.* Then he would tell her the latest report from Anu, describing the worsening conditions on Arra. But Inanna would just put her hands over her ears, closing her mind and shutting out anything anyone else told her.

In desperation, Sud went to Varda for help. "What can I do with her, Varda?" She explained how difficult Inanna was being about accepting their new life on Earth.

"I think I know just what to do," Varda said, smiling. "Sometimes seeing might be believing." She told Sud her plan. The next time Anu sent a message from Arra, Varda would invite Inanna and Utu to watch. Because Inanna adored Anu, Varda knew Inanna would believe whatever he told her. Not only that, but Inanna would finally see for herself the dreadful conditions back on Arra.

The day of the next message from Anu came after a long wait. Sud was at her wits end by now, so she held her breath while thinking, *This has to work.* Varda ushered the twins into the communication room and stood them in front of the large screen. Anu wept as he showed them the once-pink sky now a dreary gray, and his palace gardens with its lush greenery turned yellow and flowers dying. Inanna just stood there and stared at the screen, as if in shock. She said nothing to anyone. At last, her complaining ceased.

One day soon after, Eä came to discuss serious matters with Morgoth over breakfast. The situation had gone on too long in silence, and now it was time for them to talk. Eä could see that Morgoth was irritated by his presence, but he knew he had to deal with it before it festered into something viler.

"Neither of us likes being stuck here forever," Eä says. "Is there any way we can work together?"

Morgoth didn't answer the question. Instead, he spews angry words at Eä. "I gave up my whole life for Anu, and what do I get for it? This miserable frontier – and *you.*"

Despite Morgoth's undeniable resentment, Eä tries to reason with him. "Be angry at Anu, not me. We're brothers, aren't we? Not enemies."

But Morgoth only glowers at him. "What makes you think we're *brothers*? We never had the same blood, and we certainly don't have the same goals." He pauses, and then adds, "We're men now, not children."

Overwhelmed, and with a sense of futility, Eä feels too astounded to argue. He wonders if he can ever work things out with this hardened man, now a total stranger to him. *Was he ever my brother?* he wonders. He takes a deep breath, ready for one last try.

"Look, Morgoth, this is my best offer," he says. "When we go home, I'll convince Anu that I don't want your crown. You have my word."

He waits, but Morgoth only stares back with cold unfeeling eyes.

Eä goes on, "In return, I want your Igigi to help us finish the ziggurat at Larsa. After that, they can work the refineries at Bad-Tibira."

To Eä's surprise, Morgoth agrees, but then adds, "On one condition. The ziggurat at Larsa will be mine."

"Fine," Eä replies, still struggling to remain calm as memories of their boyhood rivalry flood his mind. *Same old Morgoth*, he thinks. *Nothing's changed; nothing ever will change.* With tension still evident in his voice, he says, "You can run Mission Control for me, from the ziggurat at Larsa." *That should make him happy*, he convinces himself. *Peace at any price, perhaps, but will the price be too high?* He shakes off any misgivings. *Too late now. The sooner we finish, the sooner we can leave*, he reassures himself.

In the days that followed, Eä lived to regret that decision. Eä knew in his heart that if Morgoth ever tired of being second in command, a terrible conflict would be inevitable. A battle to the death might even result, especially if Morgoth tried to seize control of Eä's men. Eä felt some relief when the Igigi arrived at Larsa to help with the construction. The work progressed more rapidly. At least, for a while.

Then the crucial day finally came, a day that changed everything. Struggling under the blazing sun, tempers suddenly flared between the two camps. One group of men was loyal to Morgoth, and the other, loyal to Eä. Morgoth gave a command to one of Eä's men over a minor incident. Eä countermanded Morgoth. Morgoth shouted back that he was in charge. Eä reminded him that Anu had removed Morgoth from command, after he had nearly destroyed Arra. Now fighting mad, Morgoth moved toward Eä with all the pent up hatred he had been holding back since losing his position as Crown Prince.

Eä's android, Bog, flashed red. Without their familiar weapons at hand, men on both sides grabbed hammers, axes, shovels, and whatever else was handy to use for a weapon. The Igigi rushed to stand behind Morgoth; the Arran heroes stood behind Eä. They hovered on the brink, inches from commencing a bloody, deadly battle.

At that moment, that Varda intervened. Still under secret orders from Anu to keep the gold coming, no matter what she had to do, she reminded Eä that saving Arra was far more important than any personal rivalry with Morgoth. With such an enormous task before them, they could not afford to lose a single man.

Eä came to his senses first, and realizing that Varda was right, he stepped back from the imminent disaster. Instead, he offered Morgoth a truce. If Morgoth wanted

Larsa, he could have it. Not only Larsa, but also the ziggurat they were constructing and all the northern territory of Earth. Eä would rule the southern territory of Earth and run the gold mines. The only condition was that Morgoth would stay in the north and leave Eä alone.

Without realizing it, Eä had just given away half the Earth. A high price to pay for a very uncertain peace with Morgoth.

Chapter 3
A WEDDING

By sixteen, Inanna had grown into a beautiful and sensual young woman. So for her sixteenth birthday, Morgoth and Sud gave an extravagant party for Inanna and her twin brother Utu at the family's luxurious palace at Larsa. They invited the entire entourage of royalty now living on Earth, but from Eä's family, only Geshtina, Lugal, and Dumuzi accepted. Marduk and his parents, hoping to avoid more ruffled feathers, made their excuses.

The spacious hall, now decorated with fresh flowers and strewn with a mountain of puffy cushions, opened into a lush garden. Inanna's still youthful mother, Sud, bustles about, fussing with streamers, garlands, and last minute arrangements. Interrupted by two servants, she turns to give them instructions on where to place their enormous trays of food, one tray laden with bite-sized pieces of freshly roasted meats and the other with luscious fruits and tiny pastries.

"Hurry," she tells the servants, "the other guests will be here soon."

On one side of the room, Inanna's older and unmarried sister, Ereshkigal, flirts with Lugal and Dumuzi, two of the most eligible candidates for a royal marriage. Lugal, now twenty, dark and powerful, has an unshaven look from a stubborn beard that resists shaving. In contrast, Eä's youngest and most pampered son, Dumuzi, although handsome and charming, is still a pink-faced and boyish eighteen.

Utu, debonair as always, laughs and talks with the others, until he notices Inanna. She stands alone, sampling dates from a table filled with tempting fruits and pastries. Inanna casts searing glances at Ereshkigal, gazing covertly through eyes masked by thick eyelashes. Her expression shows ominous disapproval.

"Something wrong, Inanna?" Utu asks, coming over to her.

"Look at Ereshkigal," she says, turning her back on her sister. "Everyone's talking to *her*." She pretends interest in the fruit while she pokes at the tray to select another date.

"So? What do you expect?" Utu asks. Then he smiles, teasing. "Are you jealous?"

"No!" she says, defending herself. But then she glances at Ereshkigal again. Moving close to Utu and turning away from Ereshkigal, she whispers, "See how she's acting with Lugal? It's disgusting." She tosses the date back on the tray. "I hope she marries him. Then Father will send her to the Kur, where she belongs."

"What about you?" Utu asks, hoping to distract her.

"Me?" she scoffs. "I'm bored! There's nothing to do here, not like it was on Arra, with all the grand parties, and dances, and…," her voice trails off. Suddenly she exclaims, "I know what we can do. You can teach me to fly!"

"Oh no," Utu says, shaking his head.

"Why not?" she demands. "You fly."

"Flying is for men, dear sister," he says. "Skybirds are dangerous."

"For me and not for you? Don't be a silly ass," she says, growing angry. "The only reason women can't fly is because no one teaches them. If I were on Arra, Anu would command someone to teach me."

"Good thing Anu isn't here," he says, teasing her. "You're sixteen now. You should be married."

"I don't want to be married!" she protests. "I want to fly, so I can go places and see things. I want to do hundreds of exciting things when I'm a queen."

He looks at her and shakes his head. "How will you ever be a queen if you don't marry?"

She sticks her tongue out at him and turns away.

He follows, grabbing her arm. "Look over there," he says, pointing to Dumuzi. "If he had his way, he'd marry you."

Inanna looks, but Dumuzi sees her. Quickly, she looks down at the food again. "Don't be silly, Utu. He's just a *boy*, and a shepherd," she says, with obvious disgust. "The man of my dreams has to be strong, with noble bearing and dignified enough to be a king. I need to find a rich man who will bring grain in great heaps to fill my storehouses each season."

Utu reaches out and touches her necklace of lapis lazuli. "You mean, like Marduk?"

Her eyes blaze with sudden anger. She recalls how smitten she had been with Marduk. He was so self-assured, and truly a man of noble bearing. He was Eä's oldest son, the one most likely to be king one day. She had flirted with him, and she was sure he would ask to marry her. How could he resist? Who else was more beautiful than she, or more connected to Morgoth's wealth and royal power? After all, *she* was Anu's granddaughter. No one ever knew how humiliated she had been when she heard from Ereshkigal that Marduk had called her a *brat*. A brat! Even worse, he called her a spoiled child who craved power, like Morgoth, and she would be the last person he would choose to marry. Even so, Inanna decided not to believe Ereshkigal.

Then she received the announcement that Marduk would marry Sarpanit. *How could he? Sarpanit is a nobody! Not even royalty. And so plain.* More insult to her already injured pride. At the wedding, watching Marduk make vows to another woman, Inanna's painful sense of rejection turned to hatred. She promised herself that no man would ever degrade her like that again. *When I'm a queen, he'll be sorry*, she promised. She'd make sure of that.

"Don't ever mention his name to me!" Inanna lashes back at Utu. "If I can't have the man I want, then I shall never marry."

"Don't be silly," Utu says, chuckling with good-natured understanding. "You are meant to marry a king, Inanna." Lifting one of the bright azure stones in her lapis lazuli necklace, he says, "I see you're still wearing these bright beads of fertility, so why pretend you're so unwilling to marry?"

"Only unwilling to marry a clod, like Dumuzi," she says, feeling strong dislike.

"What's wrong with Dumuzi?" Utu asks, feigning innocence. "Eä will give him land and make him a king one day, just like Lugal. Dumuzi has great potential."

"King or not, I will never marry anyone who raises sheep!" Inanna replies, even more petulant. "Ranchers always stink like sheep, and their clothes are made of rough wool. Can you imagine what that coarse weave of wool would do to my skin? I want only soft linen to wear. Only those luxuries that come from the soil will give me flax for my robes and the best barley for my table."

Dumuzi goes to the far end of the table where he stands sampling fruit, unnoticed. Overhearing Inanna's conversation, Dumuzi ambles over to her. Still munching on a date, he says, "So you want to marry a farmer, Inanna?"

She looks up at him, taken aback by his rude intrusion. She looks away, making an effort to ignore him.

"Tell me," Dumuzi persists, following her. "What more does a farmer have to give you?"

She remains silent and moves further away.

Determined, he pursues her. "I have wool instead of flax, sweet milk instead of beer, honey cheese instead of bread." Frowning, he grabs her by the shoulders and turns her to him, demanding an answer. "Is all that not good enough for you?"

Incensed, her face red, she removes his hands. "How dare you speak to me like that?" she exclaims. Glaring at him with contempt, she erupts, "All my relatives grow crops. Our fields are rich with flax and grain for bread. Now you dare to speak against us. Do you think you and your smelly animals are better than we are?"

Utu throws up his hands, laughing at her tirade. "Watch out, Dumuzi. She has a terrible temper."

Inanna scowls at Utu, but he grins and leaves her with her ingenuous suitor.

Dumuzi's voice softens. "Inanna, let's not quarrel about our families, or how we raise our food. We all need milk and bread, don't we? Without animals, we would have no milk. Without crops, we would have no bread. All life comes from the rich soil on this planet, from plants and the animals who eat the plants. Don't you agree?"

She gazes into his smiling face, searching her own mind for a reason to argue.

"Farmer or rancher, isn't one as good as the other?" He offers his arm to her. "Come. Walk with me. We can talk it over, in the garden."

She hesitates, and then rests her hand on his arm.

———

Outside in the garden, listening to the song of the nightingale, they find a place to sit together beside an apple tree. He takes her hand and speaks to her in a soft and seductive voice.

"Inanna, won't you visit me? Come to my orchard. We can lie beneath the apple trees and dream of the day we will plant the sweet honey-covered seed." He presses his lips to her hand.

She smiles, flattered by his youthful advances. *How innocent and decent he is, not at all as heartless and contemptible as his rotten brother, Marduk.* She says, "Your charms are sweet, Dumuzi." Teasing him with a most flirtatious smile, her voice grows soft and inviting. "I am flattered that you would invite me to your orchard and offer me the fruit of your apple tree." Then with an oblique glance, she says, "How kind of you," fluttering long eyelashes.

He gazes at her, as he would an adorable kitten, wishing to hold her close to him. "Better still to rest beside you, heart to heart." He presses her hand to his heart. She smiles to herself, suddenly sensing a conquest, a secret delight she has never known before.

———

At her palace at Larsa, Inanna and her mother, Sud, are in their private chambers while Inanna chatters away about her visit to Dumuzi. "Last night Dumuzi led me into his garden…"

Standing behind Inanna, Ninshubar, a dark-skinned servant, bathes Inanna in a luxurious sunken tub while Sud listens.

"…And we strolled through the orchard under the full moon. We listened to the song of the nightingales in the trees. I could smell the fragrance of the apple blossoms drifting on the warm night air. When he took my hand, I felt intoxicated! Then we knelt together beneath an apple tree," Inanna said, as if speaking from a vision.

Ninshubar rolls her eyes, and then begins scrubbing Inanna's back vigorously.

Ignoring Ninshubar, still in her reverie, Inanna's voice takes on a dreamy quality as she describes the events of her meeting with Dumuzi under the full moon.

Ninshubar stops scrubbing and listens, now captivated by the story.

Inanna continues, "He put his hand in mine, but then something strange happened." She drops her reverie, as if waking from a dream state, and looks over at Sud. "I don't understand it, Mother. At first, I felt nothing, so I withdrew my hand and pulled away. I expected him to stop, but instead he moved closer. When he brushed his lips against my neck… I trembled."

Sud smiles at her. "What do you think about that now?"

Ninshubar rinses the soap off Inanna's back.

Inanna considered Sud's question. "I'm not sure, but do you suppose he'll ask to marry me?"

"That's not the way a marriage is decided, Inanna," Sud cautions. "You must wait... to make sure you are not blinded by your own passion."

Ninshubar pours liquid over Inanna's hair.

As the soap bubbles up, Inanna closes her eyes. "But Mother," Inanna says, drifting back into her dreamy state, "the plants and herbs in his field are so ripe, and the fullness in his loins excites me..."

Sud frowns, her voice growing stern. "You are a princess, Inanna," Sud reminds her. "You must choose a man who will be a strong warrior king, like your father – not a shepherd boy like Dumuzi."

Inanna opens her eyes to protest. *She can't say no,* her mind shouts while her thoughts race. *Marduk has already married Sarpanit, and soon Ereshkigal will marry Lugal. One day both will become queens. No one else is left. I must convince her, I must!*

"But Mother," Inanna argues, "with my help Dumuzi will be a fine king. He'll make you proud, I'm sure of it. Besides, who else could I marry who will make me a queen?"

Seizing the perfect moment, Ninshubar pours water over Inanna's soapy head.

Inanna sputters, wiping the water from her eyes.

Ninshubar smiles and hands Inanna a towel.

Trying to reason with Inanna, Sud says, "You know we have bad blood between our families, Inanna. Eä knows we need slaves to build our canals. What will happen if he refuses to send them? You know your father. Morgoth won't allow anyone to challenge his command, not even his brother."

Inanna rises from her bath, slowly mounting the three steps leading up from the sunken tub. Water trickles down her back, over her narrow waist, and then to her bare buttocks.

Ninshubar waits on the platform, ready to wrap the firm flesh and flowing contours of that nubile body in a robe. When Inanna is dry, Ninshubar combs out the girl's long hair.

"Regardless of your feelings for Dumuzi," Sud goes on, "I'm sure trouble will follow. I fear your marriage to him would be doomed from the start."

Just then, Ninshubar tugs hard on a snarl.

Inanna grabs the comb from the servant. Frowning at her in anger, she jumps to her feet and pushes Ninshubar away. "Get away, you clumsy fool!" Inanna shouts, grabbing the bar of soap. Ninshubar rushes out, running for her life as the soap sails past her head.

Turning to Sud, her mood suddenly changed, Inanna wipes her hands and resumes their conversation. She coos in a dulcet voice, "You are wrong, Mother." Smiling, with an air of angelic confidence, Inanna says, "Our marriage will unite the families, not cause discord."

Sud knew how futile it would be to argue with Inanna. In an effort to avoid an argument, Sud looks away, but her face reveals a hint of sadness and disapproval.

Undeterred, Inanna goes to her mother and kneels. Using all her charm to persuade Sud to support her cause, she says, "Oh, Mother, surely you remember how it was to be in love!"

Sud looks down, and as the powerful memories flood her thoughts, she barely listens as Inanna chatters on.

Yes, I remember it well, Sud mused, *but not with your father*. On Arra, marriage had so little to do with love. Sud thought it would be different for her, for the young intern she had fallen in love with at nursing school. And then everything changed after Morgoth raped her. *I was lucky. I didn't get pregnant, like Varda. Varda didn't dare report the incident. Poor girl, she had no family that had influence with King Anu.*

But Sud's father did, and he went to Anu and demanded that Morgoth be punished, even exiled, for such a heinous act against an innocent nurse. Morgoth acted as if the nursing school was his private harem. Anu agreed, and Morgoth was banished to some lonely rock out in space, forever. But Morgoth's mother, Antu, argued against it. She reminded Anu of his treaty with Arkonia, with his promise that Morgoth would inherit Anu's throne one day, and that banishing Morgoth would break the treaty and bring down the wrath of Arkonia.

So Sud became a *peace cow*, a woman married to an enemy to preserve Anu's treaty with Arkonia. After a suitable time, Morgoth returned to Arra on the condition that he would marry Sud. She knew Morgoth was not happy about it. Even worse, after they were married, Morgoth had insisted that she should accept Ninurta, Varda's bastard son. Ninurta was to live in their home and was to be raised as their child. *What could I say? What could I do? Nothing. It was Anu's will.*

"Dumuzi is the light of the moon and the warmth of the sun," Inanna gushes.

Sud looks up suddenly, returning from distant memories.

"There will be no other for me, not ever. Please, Mother. Let the marriage be prepared. They say that nothing is sweeter than the bed that brings honey to the loins. Is that not true, Mother?"

She gazes at Inanna with concern, and then strokes her youthful face with a gentle hand. "If it's what you want, my dearest daughter, the marriage will be prepared."

Inanna jumps up and hugs Sud with a squeal of delight, then twirls around with joy. "I'm so happy, Mother. At last, I will be a queen!"

Sud gazes at her daughter's naiveté with a sense of deep foreboding.

———

At Morgoth's palace at Larsa, Inanna's wedding day finally arrives. Several chattering young women help to put final touches on Inanna as they prepare for the ceremony. When the jittery Inanna is finally ready for the ceremony,

Dumuzi's timid ten-year-old sister, Geshtina, comes over to her and kisses her cheek.

"I hope you make Dumuzi happy, Inanna," Geshtina says. "I'm going to miss him," the little girl breaks off. Tears well in her eyes.

Inanna gazes at her. "Don't be silly, Geshtina," Inanna scolds. "You won't lose him."

"But he's going away," Geshtina blurts, tears running down her cheeks. "Forever."

"Stop that," Inanna orders. She takes her own handkerchief and dabs away the girl's tears. "He's still your brother. I'll always love his whole family as my own, especially you."

Geshtina looks up at the beautiful Inanna with adoration. "Really?"

"Really," Inanna says. "I promise."

Music signals the time for Inanna's entrance. The older women grow agitated and bustle about the bride. Quickly forming a procession, they shove Geshtina to the front of the line. The girl leads the procession to the altar, sprinkling rose petals along the way. When they reach the altar, Inanna and Dumuzi join hands before Nanche, the priestess.

"Who gives this woman to be wedded?" Nanche asks.

Morgoth and Sud step forward. Inanna's brother Utu joins them.

Morgoth says, "I am Inanna's father. Her mother and brother join me to give our blessings to this marriage.

May Inanna and Dumuzi link our two families in peace and contentment."

Nanche asks, "Who gives this man to be wedded?"

Eä and Damkina step forward. Dumuzi's brothers, Lugal and Marduk, move beside them.

"I am Dumuzi's father," says Eä. His mother and brothers join me to bless and honor this marriage. May his bride dwell with our family in peace and contentment."

Nanche turns to Dumuzi and asks, "Dumuzi, what vows do you make to Inanna?"

Dumuzi takes Inanna's hands in his and gazes at her with love. "My beautiful Inanna," he says, "I promise to care for you and protect you forever. All that I have, I give to you, now and always, for all our days."

Nanche wraps their wrists together with a golden cord. Then she closes her eyes. "O Sky and Sea," she implores, lifting her arms in supplication, "carry this tender love into that immortal kingdom beyond this world and let the stars bind their hearts forever."

Geshtina brings a silver tray with two tiny cakes and a small crystal goblet of wine. Inanna and Dumuzi feed each other cake and wine. Nanche wraps the empty goblet in a fine linen cloth and puts it on the floor.

Grinning with delight, Dumuzi shatters the glass with his foot. The crowd cheers. Dumuzi takes Inanna into his arms and kisses her with passion.

Lively music signals the celebration to begin.

The crowd forms a circle around the couple, clapping to the music. Dumuzi and Inanna join the circle and dance with the others in joyous celebration.

———

Later that night, Lugal and Marduk are alone in the great banquet hall preparing the table for the wedding feast. While the sounds of music, dancing, and laughter drift in from the noisy wedding celebration, they hide beads and squares of lapis lazuli under a heap of dates near Inanna's place at the table.

When the music stops, Marduk whispers to Lugal, "Hurry! They're coming." They scurry away, laughing in anticipation of her surprise at their prank.

Inanna and the others enter the hall in a loud and jovial mood. The two families sit at the banquet table on large couches and pillows. While servants pour wine and bring in huge platters of food for the guests, Inanna samples the dates in front of her.

Suddenly, she notices the precious stones, the beads and squares of lapis lazuli.

"Oh!" she gasps with delight. "Look, Dumuzi, lapis lazuli!" She holds up one of the squares for all to see. "Isn't it gorgeous?" One at a time, she passes each of the brilliant azure stones to Dumuzi, for him to admire.

Morgoth rises and lifts his goblet of wine. The group grows quiet.

"On this joyful day, let us put all past differences behind us," Morgoth says. Now that we have linked our two families together in a bond of love and respect, let us all offer our blessings to the marriage of Inanna and Dumuzi."

They all drink a toast, "To Inanna and Dumuzi!" Then they laugh and applaud the couple. Music strikes up and everyone eats and drinks in celebration.

Still holding his goblet, Morgoth goes over to Eä and sits beside him, smiling as graciously as he can. "How fares the mining, *Brother*?" he asks.

"All is well in the Abzu," Eä responds, wondering about Morgoth calling him *brother*. Despite his skepticism, Eä tries to remain genial. "And you?" he asks, with formal politeness.

"We're finally getting our canals built," Morgoth replies. "We need to prevent flooding of our cities, but the labor is difficult." Morgoth signals a servant to refill his wine. He sips the wine, and calmly adds, "I'll soon require more workers."

Eä pauses. *And there it is*, Eä thinks, gazing at the reflections in his wine. Without missing a beat, he replies, "Rest easy, Morgoth." Then with veiled meaning, he adds, "We'll do our best to fill all your needs."

Morgoth smiles and tips his goblet to acknowledge Eä's apparent good will.

Just then, a commotion in the background interrupts their conversation. Everyone turns to look. They watch as Inanna and Dumuzi escape to their bedroom amid a shower of rose petals, while the crowd laughs and cheers.

"Let's hope they'll always be as happy as they are to-night," Eä says.

"Let's just hope they can endure," Morgoth adds, with his usual sour and unsmiling face.

———

In the honeymoon bedroom that same night, Dumuzi comes up behind Inanna and fondles her breasts. Slowly, he removes her wedding garments. She responds to his kisses with passion, eager to consummate their union. At last, he lifts her onto the bed.

"You are as soft as rose petals," he says, nestling his face near her breasts. "Your beauty intoxicates me, simple shepherd that I am."

As though his words have awakened a deeper passion, her eyes open wide. "You can be more than a shepherd if you want to," she says, running her finger along his lips. "Your sweet mouth suits you, prince that you are. You have the divine light of Anu's great power, so you should hold your head high. In all ways, you're meant to sit on a throne and wear a royal crown, dress in long robes, and adorn yourself with a king's scepter."

Unaffected by her flattery, he replies, "I need no titles or royal symbols." Aroused, he moves toward her. With a voice heavy with passion, he breathes, "I want only to love you."

She puts her fingers on his lips, holding him back. "Wait, my dearest. First, let me tell you of my dream."

Although slightly chilled by the rebuff, he holds off, listening.

"I saw you subdue a great nation of rebellious people," she says, in lofty tones. "They chose you as ruler of their country. After you conquered that nation, I directed it and gave you status. If you could do this for me, I'd make the name Dumuzi glorious. Think of it!"

Dumuzi smiles, as if she's only teasing again. "Let's not think of ruling nations tonight, my beautiful Inanna. I'm content to bask in your glorious love." Once more, he grows passionate, but still she holds him off.

"We must think of it!" she demands. "Especially tonight."

"Why tonight?" he asks, still smiling, still patient. "This our wedding night."

"Silly goose!" she blurts. "For love to last, we must act together in all things."

He pursues her with little kisses down her nude torso. "If that will please you, then I'll conquer a thousand nations and make them worship at your feet."

"If you do that for me, beloved, I'll worship you forever." She smiles at her victory.

He disappears under the covers, busy between her thighs.

She relaxes to enjoy his foreplay, but unable to resist yet another thought, she says, "Promise me."

This time, he can wait no longer. He mutters, "I promise," and enters her with great command.

She gasps with delight. All thoughts leave her mind, and she surrenders her body to the magic of the moment.

Chapter 4
RETRIBUTION

Although Eä had sent regular shipments of gold to Arra, Anu had observed little change in the Rift. The daylight sky was still an ominous gray over the royal palace at Astra. Worried, Anu contacted Earth on his space communicator.

"The hole is still there," Anu said. "Despite all the gold you sent, the Rift doesn't seem to be closing. Nothing has changed."

"Be patient, Father," Eä said, to calm him. "We need many tons of gold just to slow the churning. Even more to shrink the hole."

Still anxious, Anu asks, "Will you have enough gold?"

"There's more than enough gold on Earth," Eä said. "We'll find a new lode as soon as we need it." Then he added, "Don't worry. As long as Morgoth is occupied in the north, I can focus all my efforts on mining gold now."

Eä was not aware that his anxious father had already usurped his command of the mines. Lacking confidence in Eä, Anu wanted to make certain the miners did not desert their duty. So Anu instructed Morgoth to send Igigi guards to Eä's mines in the south, thus nullifying the agreement Eä had made for Morgoth to stay north and leave Eä to run the mines in the south.

When Anu told Eä what he had done, Eä could not believe he had heard correctly. Confronted, Anu justified his actions by stating that Arra had never faced such a dire situation before. "A king must do what a king must do," Anu had said, resorting to his favorite maxim.

Eä could not accept Anu's excuse. To Eä, nothing could justify such actions. "Don't you realize what you've done, Father?" he asked. "Our miners are honorable men. They volunteered to risk their lives to save Arra. Now Morgoth will treat them like criminals."

"Nonsense," Anu argued. "Gold is far too important to us now to let the men defect."

Eä could not control his outrage. He shouted, "I don't want Morgoth or his Igigi anywhere near my mines!"

But Anu refused to back down. Patronizing Eä, he said, "Should the miners get unruly, my boy, you'll welcome Morgoth's help. My orders stand."

And that was that.

———

Time dragged on at the mines. The men were exhausted, and yet they worked on. The hard grind was bad enough, but when Morgoth sent Ninurta, the Enforcer, to impose strict discipline at the mines, the situation became intolerable for the miners. They called a strike and refused to work. Ninurta announced that if they didn't meet their quota of ore, he would withhold food until they did. A terrible mutiny followed. The miners jumped from the pit and took Ninurta hostage. Eä arrived just in time to stop Ninurta's guards from slaughtering the unarmed miners with laser rifles.

Eä knew in his heart that his men were heroes, and they didn't deserve to be branded forever as mutinous cowards and killers. And where would they go? For now, Arra was still dying. Gold was Arra's only hope. If the miners mutinied, no home would be waiting for them. If they stayed, and if Arra survived this tragedy, they could go home later as true heroes.

Eä promised the men relief, better food, and no more guards standing over them with rifles. Finally, he gave his word that replacements would be on the way. *Where will we ever find replacements?* he had wondered. Nevertheless, to his relief the miners agreed to continue work, but only until the replacements arrived. To bind Eä to his promise, they kept Ninurta hostage, a powerful but unspoken threat. Eä knew they would kill Ninurta if he broke his word. Then what? With great certainty, he could predict what outcome that would bring. Morgoth would retaliate. He'd send the Igigi on a mission to kill all the miners, or even lead them himself. With that, all hope for Arra would evaporate. It would be the end of his world.

How much time do I have? he wondered. *How long will the miners wait?* He didn't know. Then a silly little idea first flashed into his mind. *What would happen if we cloned the miners?* Immediately, he dismissed the notion as foolish. Instead, he called Anu and reported what had happened at the mines. "I promised the miners replacements," Eä had said. He told Anu that Ninurta was their hostage, and if replacements didn't come soon, a bloody mutiny would arise immediately after they killed Ninurta.

Then Eä said, "I don't know where we'll find enough men, unless I clone the miners that are here."

"Clone Arrans?" Anu exploded. "Our law forbids it!"

"Then what else can we do?" Eä asked.

After serious thought, Anu said, "If you're that desperate, I'll send five thousand men from Arra right now."

Eä argued that those men might be needed on Arra if the planet had to be evacuated, but as far as Anu was concerned, the issue was closed. Replacements would be on the way.

———

Eä went back to work, content that Anu would keep his word. When he told the miners that five thousand replacements were in transit, they cheered. Ninurta would be happy to return to Larsa. The crisis was over.

Then the horrible news came.

Eä burst into the clinic, "They're dead!" he shouted to Varda. "All of them."

At first, she didn't understand why he was shouting. She just stared at him and waited. Seeing her puzzled frown, he calmed down. Then he reported to her that the starship from Arra had just entered Earth's galaxy when it was struck by a huge asteroid. The direct hit exploded the anti-matter engine, annihilating the ship and everyone aboard.

At once, she realized that Ninurta was in more danger than before. The situation had changed so quickly. A few moments ago, she believed the danger was over. Now it was worse than ever. When she finally grasped the enormous consequences hanging over them, anxiety flooded her mind. She had never felt so helpless. "What will you do?" she asked.

Eä gazed at her with tortured eyes. "All I can think of is cloning replacements."

"You know that's not an option," she murmured. "It's forbidden."

"I know the law forbids cloning Arrans," he reasoned, "but it's not a violation to clone these natives. We could enhance their essence with our own."

A heated discussion concerning Arran law and their ethical responsibilities followed. At one point, Lugal jumped in, adding fuel to the fire. He raged at them, pointing out that the Aeons would curse them all if they dared contaminated the Arran Code of Life. Eä had looked at him with an irritated glance, the way he might observe an annoying insect, and then turned back to Varda. She thought Eä's plan was selfish; he thought his plan was altruistic, devoted to the benefit of everyone involved.

After listening to the long argument between Eä and Varda, Lugal could remain silent no longer. Feeling left out, with anger mounting, he growled at Eä, "You think you're so smart, but your idea is just plain stupid!"

The comment hung in the air. Eä took a step toward Lugal in a rage, as if to strike him. Varda called out to him just in time. Eä stopped. "Get out of my sight, boy," he commanded Lugal. "Go to the mines and do something useful."

They waited while Lugal stomped out, and then Varda turned to Eä. "Cloning would only be trial and error," she said. "We might never get it right."

"But the challenge, Varda," he urged. "Think of it."

"I have," she replied. "I don't think it's possible."

———

Caught between the growing emergency on Arra and the threat of mutiny at the mines, Varda knew they had to make a choice. She remembered Anu's command, *Do whatever you have to do, but keep the gold coming.* She searched for a solution. *What about Ninurta?* she wondered. *They'll kill him!* She was certain of that, once they found out there would be no replacements. So she decided to accept Eä's plan. At least she could begin exploring the possibility of a prototype, as difficult as even that might be.

In the meantime, Eä called the miners together and told the dreadful story of how five thousand replacements had been annihilated. He explained that Varda was attempting to clone more workers using the natives, but it was too soon to know whether she would be successful. It would take more time to produce a suitable prototype, and after the clones were born, the miners would have to wait fifteen years until the clones were old enough to work the mines. Since one Arran shar was equivalent to thirty-six hundred Earth years, the miners understood that fifteen Earth years was only a blip on the Arran scale of time.

So they waited. They even released Ninurta. Although Eä felt relieved that the miners supported his plan, he knew their support was mainly because Morgoth's Igigi were gone. Heroes, such as these men were, rarely make a sacrifice only because guns are pointed at them. The Igigi did not seem to understand that principle, since the Igigi responded only to power. Strangely enough, the mutiny had united the miners. They had all come together into one mind, one effort, and one task: save Arra.

Time passed. After much trial and error, Eä and Varda created the Adamu, a prototype capable of learning how to do what was required. At last, the first clones were born, with the help of the nurses who volunteered to be surrogate mothers. When the clones were mature, at about fifteen years, they became the first replacements, as promised. After Varda developed her cloning techniques, she was able to duplicate the process repeatedly, thus producing a steady supply of clones to replace the miners.

——

Back on Arra, the advisors feared a growing panic due to the Rift. They advised Anu, "Tour the cities, talk to the people, and try to calm them."

Anu exploded at them in frustration, shouting, "Calm them! How? With empty promises?" He had never dealt with anything like this before, had never dreamed he would ever have to deal with such unthinkable happenings on such a large scale. *I'm their king*, he reminded himself. *My job is to get us past this crisis. But how can I, without all the gold that Eä promised?"*

"Contact Morgoth," Anu had said, turning back to his advisors. "Tell him I want to know what's holding up the gold shipments."

"Sire," one advisor said, with caution. "Morgoth already told us that he can't process more gold until he adds extra smelters."

"First it's the mines, now it's the smelters," Anu fumed. "What next? We'll all be dead if that gold doesn't get here soon!"

——

Whatever news came to Sud about the mutiny at Eä's mines, or about the Rift on Arra, did not seem to interest her daughter. Inanna simply closed her ears to it all, as if determined not to let anything spoil her life with Dumuzi. Even though Inanna saw nothing of her father, she did not seem to miss living with him. Sud told her that Morgoth and Ninurta were away most of the time, off building smelters somewhere in the north. *Such a relief with Morgoth away*, Sud told herself. She had tired of his bad temper a long time ago, and even though she felt lonely at times, she was content to be alone.

Several reports had come to Sud from Arra. Apparently, the people were growing sick, and for the first time since leaving Arra, Sud was glad to be living on Earth. She read that in the city of Astra alone, people were lining up outside the hospitals, some gagging and others unable to stop retching. The emergency rooms had filled with weak or terminal patients. Others lined the hospital halls on gurneys, waiting with oozing sores and peeling skin for whatever medical attention they could get from the limited staff. It was reported that Anu was distraught. No one seemed to know what to do.

Thinking now of Morgoth, Sud froze. *There will be terrible pressure from Anu*, she realized. She knew from experience that pressure from Anu led to Morgoth's angry outbursts, outbursts that were directed at anyone and anything around him. *Thank the Aeons that Morgoth is still in Bad-Tibira*, she told herself.

The comfort she felt at Morgoth's absence did not last long. A few days later, Morgoth blustered into the house, unannounced, like a violent storm. Ninurta followed behind him, like a well-trained hound. Sud bustled into action to make him comfortable, bringing him wine, and then arranging for a splendid dinner of his favorite meats and fowls, and fresh-baked breads.

After dinner, Morgoth seemed relaxed. He was content to settle himself before a fire and sip his favorite green wine, a syrupy concoction made from fermented green berries grown only on Arkonia. Sud sat nearby, quiet as usual, concentrating on her tapestry.

"Anu keeps pressuring me," Morgoth says.

She looks up, surprised that he might confide in her. *What mischief are you up to now?* she wonders.

"We need more men or we'll never make the next shipment," Morgoth says, talking to himself more than to Sud. He grows quiet for a while, and then continues thinking aloud. "If only we could get some of Eä's clones. Ninurta thinks Eä must have hundreds of them by now."

"Have you asked him?" Sud says, daring to question him even though she knows the answer. *He wouldn't be so troubled if he thought Eä would comply*, she thought.

"I sent Ninurta," he says. "Eä knows we need more clones to work the smelters."

Of course, he knows, Sud muses, *and of course, Eä will refuse*. "What will you do if Eä denies your request?"

"Request!" Morgoth roars at Sud. "I'm not asking, I'm ordering. If he refuses, we'll take the clones. Like it or not."

Sud stares at him, astonished. *You fool!* she thinks. *Eä will never let you take his clones. If you interfere, you risk the lives of all our people on Arra. It might even start a war with Eä.*

"What about Anu?" she asks. "Eä will tell him, won't he?"

"Let him," Morgoth sneers. "Anu wants gold, doesn't he? It's my job to deliver it. Eä just wants me to look bad."

If Eä is refusing to give you his clones just to make you look bad, you must be losing your mind! Sud proceeds with caution, "Is it worth the risk?"

"Call it the price of winning," he replies.

"Winning?" she asks, puzzled.

He gives her a twisted smile, the kind she recognizes as his way of masking some secret plan. "If it makes Anu realize that I should be king and not Eä, then so be it."

———

Inanna still has not given Dumuzi an heir, even after more than five shars of marriage. In frustration, she approaches Dumuzi while he is at play with one of his lambs in their garden. *Look at him*, she thinks, *spending more time with those lambs than with me.*

"Why are you playing with those stupid animals?" she asks, her voice harsh and contemptuous.

Dumuzi looks up at her with sad eyes.

"You always have your lambs," she carps, "but what about me? I still have no son to hold."

"It's not that we haven't tried," he says. He shrugs. "Perhaps we are destined to be childless."

"I'm tired of your excuses," she says. "We're not doomed to this as our destiny. Not when you can still have a son by your half-sister."

"No, I can't." He returns to playing with the lamb.

But she persists. "Have you no pride?" she demands, standing over him.

"You know Geshtina rejected me," he says. "Let's speak of it no more."

She gazes down at him. "A strong king *must* have an heir. Otherwise, who will continue your line?" She waits.

He says nothing.

Even more frustrated, she challenges him. "Are you a man, or a child? Go back to her," she commands, "and this time, don't take no for an answer."

"Don't you understand?" Dumuzi argues. "She'll refuse."

"So? Do as Enlil once did," she instructs. "Claim your right by the ancient laws." Inanna tries to restrain her impatience. She muses, *He may be content to be a poor shepherd all his life, but he was born to be a king. He doesn't think of his destiny, or of mine. If he should die without a son or daughter, what would happen to me? I'd never be a queen if that happened.*

"It's wrong," he insists. "She's my sister."

"Your half-sister," she says, correcting him. *Is he a dolt? Surely, he knows that a son born by the half-sister of a king will have priority in the succession.*

Long ago, the Arrans decided that the purity of a king or queen's lineage must be taken into account. Purity of noble blood took precedence over even birth order. Since Arrans were concerned with preserving the sacred attributes of their royal line, they reasoned that a child born from the union of a brother and a half-sister, would be "by the blood" and therefore more royal. The child would be "more king" or "more queen" than one born from an "outsider" of the family. For this type of union to be pure, the mating could be by the same father, but to avoid the possibility of congenital defects, the union must have a different mother. Therefore, it was perfectly legitimate for Geshtina and Dumuzi to produce an heir, since Geshtina was Eä's daughter by a palace concubine called Ninsun, and Dumuzi was Eä's son by Damkina. They had the same father, but different mothers.

"We've waited long enough," Inanna says. "Just take her. It's your right."

Dumuzi eyes grow wide with shock. As he comprehends her meaning, he appears stricken. "No!" he exclaims. "I cannot."

Inanna loses patience with him. "Once you promised to conquer a thousand nations and make them worship at my feet," she rails, her tone heavy with accusation. "Now you flinch at this simple thing. Perhaps my mother was right – you're unfit to walk with pride among the kings of my family!"

He stares at her in disbelief, as if she is a stranger to him.

She goes on. "Without a son, you have no honor and no place in history. Your name will be erased from the tablets. Is that what you want?"

He grows silent and sad, tormented by indecision. Pondering, he fondles the lamb with loving caresses. Heaving a great sigh, he submits. "Very well," he replies, dejected, "if it pleases you."

But giving in to Inanna's harsh demands brings him no relief. His sense of shame is so great that he cannot look at her. He turns away from her and sends the lamb out into the pasture. Watching the lamb run off, he says, "I'll go now."

———

Dumuzi is shepherding his flock in a remote tree-lined pasture when he looks up. He sees Geshtina in the distance coming toward him. She is smiling, walking carefree and relaxed, with a harp slung over her shoulder. She waves to him. Waving back, he realizes that she is only seventeen, a naïve young girl who knows nothing of men. His heart grows heavy at the prospect of what Inanna has ordered him to do.

"Dumuzi," Geshtina calls, reaching out to him. "What a wonderful day for a picnic! I'm so happy you invited me."

She gives him an affectionate hug. "We spend so little time together," she chides. "I thought you had forgotten your little sister."

"Maybe we should do this more often," he replies. "Wait until you see what I brought for our picnic."

She sits on his blanket while he spreads out slices of cold roast chicken, apples, grapes, and baked bread dripping with honey-butter. "Oh, how wonderful!" she exclaims. "But you spoil me with all this delicious food. What are we celebrating?"

"Never mind," he says, pouring her a cup of bubbling ale. "Here, just for you. A special drink for my special sister."

She sips the ale. "Mmmm," she says. She tastes the food, then licks her fingers and drinks more ale. "I love being here with you again." She gazes out into the pasture. "Remember how we played in this pasture when I was little?" she asks.

Dumuzi grins, "Yes. You teased me by scaring away my sheep."

She giggles like a little girl again. Then she grabs her harp and plucks the strings. "Remember this song?" she asks, and then sings to him in her sweet voice.

Put to sleep your little eyes,
Set my hand upon your brow,
Listen to my dreamy song,
Let me banish all your cares.

He leans back and listens, smiling. "I remember it well. Mother used to sing me to sleep with that song. I love to hear you sing it."

Soon both of them are tipsy and in a happy mood. When she stops to sip the last of her ale, he touches her shoulder.

She looks up at him.

"Look over there," he says, pointing.

Curious, she turns to look where he points. Out in the field she sees two young lambs copulating.

While she watches, Dumuzi nuzzles against her, as if imitating the lambs.

She studies his face, but she is confused, not able to understand. *Should I laugh?* she wonders. *Or play some kind of game?*

He persists, playfully at first. Then suddenly, he grasps her wrists and forces her down on the blanket.

She looks at him with surprise, wondering what kind of game this might be.

Then he holds her there, pressing her down with the full weight of his body.

"What are you doing?" she demands, no longer amused.

Offering no explanation, he pulls up her skirt and begins fondling her.

"Let me go!" she shouts, pushing him away.

But he holds her wrists firmly, determined to mount her.

"Stop it, Dumuzi," she yells.

Now in the height of his own passion, he ignores her demands. Her struggle only fans the flames of his lust. He pushes inside her.

She screams out to him, "No! No!"

Fully aroused, he persists to climax, flooding her with his seed.

She is silent, unmoving beneath him.

Believing he has pleased her, he is content with his success. Then, when sanity returns, he tries to kiss her to express his gratitude.

"You disgraced me," she whispers, as tears of shame trickle from her eyes. "Get off!"

Startled by her anger, he dismounts and releases her.

She sits up, rigid, almost paralyzed with shock and disbelief.

"You are not disgraced, Geshtina," he says, stroking her mask-like face and straightening her hair in an attempt to make amends. In an effort to explain, he says, "Inanna told me that this is my right, since you must bear a son for us to carry on my name."

Geshtina stares at him, too wounded to believe his purpose. She quickly gathers herself and runs away, like a frightened rabbit.

Dumuzi watches her escape. He gazes after her, feeling ashamed and utterly remorseful.

———

In bed with Inanna later that night, Dumuzi wakens from a nightmare, screaming out in terror. His cry wakens Inanna.

"What is it?" she asks, still half asleep.

He sits up and holds his head, weeping. "A horrible nightmare," he whimpers. "An eagle and a vulture came here. One by one, they took away everything I owned, all my valuables. They stole every object that signified status. I tried to run away from them, but in the end, I saw myself lying dead in the pasture, among the sheep, covered with dung."

She draws him to her, resting his head on her shoulder. "Just a dream," she whispers, trying to soothe his fears.

"Yes, I know," he says. Suddenly he sits up, frightened. "But what does it mean?"

"Nothing," she says, growing impatient with his weakness. "What you did was within your rights."

"No!" he protests. "Not if it was against her will." He buries his head in his hands again. "I can still hear her screaming, begging me to stop."

"If she bears you a son, none of that will matter," she reasons. "Go back to sleep."

No sooner do they settle back in bed than they hear loud pounding on the front door. They both sit up in bed, startled.

A group of six uniformed soldiers barge into their bedroom. "Dumuzi, you're under arrest!" a brutish officer shouts.

Inanna climbs out of bed, wrapping a robe about her naked body. Outraged, she confronts the men. "By what right do you come here? Dumuzi has done nothing wrong."

Despite Inanna's protests, the officer ignores her and signals two soldiers to drag the naked Dumuzi from bed. They chain him in handcuffs and fetters.

"Prince Marduk commands us," the officer answers.

"Marduk! He has no right to act here." Inanna grows fierce. "Release Dumuzi!" she commands the soldiers.

Utu, in officer's uniform, strides into the bedroom and sees Dumuzi in chains. Faced with Inanna's ferocity, the soldiers turn to Utu for direction.

Inanna goes to her brother. "Utu! Look what they've done," she says, appealing to him for help. "Tell them to release Dumuzi at once."

Utu gazes at her, feeling trapped. Utu turns to the soldiers. "Remove his shackles," he orders. After the soldiers obey, Utu says, "Wait outside."

Utu turns to Dumuzi. "I assume you know why the soldiers are here," he says, his tone stern and accusing.

"Yes, I know." Dumuzi turns away, shivering and humiliated in his nakedness.

At once, Inanna brings him a robe and helps him into it.

Covered, Dumuzi turns back to Utu. "We're family, aren't we? Let me escape, I beg you!"

"What good would that do?" Utu demands.

"Utu, you can't take him away," Inanna entreats. "Marduk has no right..."

Utu frowns at her, knowing she would never understand the duty he must fulfill as an officer. "This is the Abzu, Inanna," he says. "Marduk has every right to act for Eä, and for Geshtina. I would do the same for you if you had been violated."

Inanna stares at Utu in bewilderment, not able to comprehend how he could compare her to Geshtina in any way. Confused by her tangled thoughts, she entreats him. "Utu, please."

Utu stands resolute, but knowing he could never resist Inanna's wide and pleading eyes, he falters. He turns to Dumuzi, angry for what Dumuzi had done and angry with himself for succumbing to Inanna's whims.

Utu tells Dumuzi, "I'm doing this because my sister asked me to help you. The best I can do is take you to Marduk. Let him decide what to do with you."

————

So Utu delivered Dumuzi to Marduk at the clone compound. Overwhelmed with shame, Dumuzi begged Marduk not to tell Eä what he had done, but Marduk knew that Geshtina had already told Eä. He explained why he could not grant Dumuzi's plea, but that only made Dumuzi feel worse.

Marduk pointed out that Dumuzi had to face a more real danger: Morgoth. Knowing that Morgoth would demand the death penalty, Marduk asked Utu not to tell Morgoth what Dumuzi had done. He also told Utu not to inform Morgoth that Dumuzi was now at the clone compound, in Eä's territory.

Unaware that Morgoth had already sent Ninurta to steal the clones from Eä's compound, neither Marduk nor Utu realized that they had placed Dumuzi in an even greater danger by trying to save him from Morgoth's wrath. The Moirai must have been laughing.

Ninurta came with his men at dawn, a time when the rest of the world was asleep. They shattered the walls around the compound with a sonic machine, and then stormed through walls and into the compound where the clones were sleeping. Terrified clones fled from the building, screaming.

Still half asleep, Marduk's guards rushed out at the first sounds of the commotion. They tried to stop the fleeing clones, but the clones were like senseless wild animals. The stampede was uncontrollable.

As the frantic clones dashed outside through broken walls, Ninurta's men herded them into the clearing around the compound. A massive transporter hovered overhead, ready to beam the stolen clones aboard.

Dumuzi rushed out into the clearing where he joined Marduk's men, who were already defending the compound. Seeing the clones about to be beamed up into the transporter, Marduk's men began shooting up at the hovering vehicle with only their handheld Smiters. Dumuzi drew his weapon and began firing.

Men in the transporter fired back with one huge microwave burst. Smiters were no match for a single burst of microwaves that could easily fry a platoon of men.

Dumuzi convulsed and fell dead beside the other men who had unwisely fired at the transporter. Sadly, the desperate action taken by those courageous souls was doomed to failure. That brave-but-futile attempt did not stop Ninurta from stealing almost the entire workforce housed in the compound. Morgoth's plan had succeeded.

Dirty and bloodstained, Marduk carried Dumuzi's body back home to Eä. It was a miserable task to take his dead brother back to his unsuspecting parents, even more so because he felt Dumuzi's death was his fault. He saw the look on Eä's face, saw his tears, felt his father's grief when Eä collapsed into his arms, wracked with sobs. He heard his mother howl when she saw the body, watched her try to console her dead son.

Then Damkina turned her wrath on Eä. "This is your fault!" she shouted. "I'll never forgive you for this, not as long as I live.

Then Lugal said, "Marduk let Dumuzi be slaughtered. It's his fault."

The blame heaped upon the guilt he already felt was too painful for Marduk. He lunged at Lugal and the two grappled on the floor.

"Stop it!" Eä commanded. "Your brother gave his life for us. Is this how you respect him?" His sons stared at him. "Even now Morgoth gloats, hoping Dumuzi's death will crush us. This is what he wants, for us to fight among ourselves."

Then Eä commanded Lugal to go to Eridu. He told him to move Anu's weapons to their hidden fortress in the Kur. These were the seven forbidden weapons Anu had given him for protection in the event of a dire emergency. They were to be used only against an enemy, but never against their own kind.

Eä looked at Lugal. "Make sure no one follows you." His next words became a warning as he delivered a final order to Lugal. "Guard them with your life."

———

At Dumuzi's funeral pyre, Utu and five soldiers carry Dumuzi's body on a bier and place it on the top of the funeral pyre. With a blazing torch, Utu lights the funeral pyre under Dumuzi's body. He steps back to join the soldiers. Eä, Damkina, and Marduk, stand as a group with Marduk's wife, Sarpanit, and their teenage son, Nabu. As the flames rise up around the body, Damkina convulses with tears for her son.

Broken and numb with grief, Inanna stands on the other side of the pyre. The only person to comfort her is her servant, Ninshubar. Inanna mutters to herself, as if speaking to Ninshubar, "All that I dreamed of accomplishing is gone now. They destroyed the one person dear to me. Instead of Dumuzi's child, I am left with an insatiable gnawing in my womb, like an unborn creature already hungry for the milk of vengeance."

Watching the flames lick at Dumuzi's body, devouring him, Ninshubar bows her head and weeps. Beside her, filled with the gnawing hatred of her inner beast, Inanna glares across the flames at Marduk and his family. With dancing firelight reflecting in her eyes, she snarls, "I curse you, Marduk."

Ninshubar looks over at Inanna in dread, at the utter hatred that has replaced Inanna's grief.

The flames leap higher, enveloping Dumuzi's body. Inanna gazes at the smoke rising up into the sky as she whispers a prayer. "Let the flames of my beloved carry this plea to the heavens. O Celestial Fates, punish the vile deed that plucked this sweet life too soon."

Inanna stands in the golden glow of the fire's reflection, her long hair blown by the fire's wind. She appears to transform, looking more like an evil goddess of vengeance. Now, as night descends, she stares across the roaring flames at Marduk.

"Hear me, O Great Ones," continuing her supplication to the three powerful spinners of Destiny. "Grant me vengeance, I beseech you. Bring death to Marduk!"

Chapter 5
SEDUCTION

Heartbroken and lonely, Inanna mopes on the banks of a river. She sits beneath an apple tree, dreaming of the days when Dumuzi courted her. Then she remembers the harsh reality that he will never be with her again. Tears flood her eyes. She buries her face in her arms and sobs.

Sud finds her there. "My little Inanna, you look so sad," she says, taking pity on her grieving daughter. Sud sits beside Inanna on the grass, watching the girl sit up and gaze down into the deep water. Worried, Sud says, "What's troubling you, my dearest? Maybe I can help."

Inanna gazes into the depths of the river with a faraway look. Her eyes seem haunted, as if visualizing another dimension of space and time.

Sud waits for her to speak, churning with worry, seeing telltale signs in her daughter that only a mother can see. *I fear she intends to drown herself in the river,* Sud thinks.

At last, Inanna begins to speak. "I've been asking the river for a reason to live, but I hear no answer." With a note of tragedy in her voice, she moans, "Now I will never be a queen."

"Is *that* all?" Sud says, relieved to hear that suicide is not the issue. Then she reaches out to touch Inanna's shoulder. "Dumuzi is gone, and that cannot be changed. My dearest, now you must accept your fate."

"I won't accept it!" Inanna insists.

Sud was used to dealing with Inanna's stubborn will, but now she proceeds with care. "Use reason, Inanna," Sud says. "Without a son, all your claims to queenship died with Dumuzi." Sud pauses, and then states, "I'd make you a queen, if I could."

Inanna looks up at her mother with sudden interest. "You could do that?"

"No, but Anu could," Sud says. "Of course, all the available kingdoms in the north have already been given to others."

Inanna turns away, sinking back into depression.

"Only the Indus Valley remains," Sud adds, attempting to soften the girl's disappointment. "Of course, it's such a barren place. No one would want it."

Inanna brightens once more. "Do you suppose Anu would make me Queen of the Indus?"

Sud laughs aloud. Humoring her daughter, she says, "Come now, Inanna. You lack the knowledge to be a queen." *Especially of weapons and the art of warfare*, Sud reminds herself. "How could you acquire the secrets contained in the Codices? Knowledge and training is essential, if you ever expect to rule."

Inanna looks at Sud, with the wildest dreams lifting her from the doldrums. "Suppose I had the Codices, Mother. Then I could ask Anu to rule the Indus, couldn't I?" she asks, sudden excitement dancing in her eyes.

Sud strokes Inanna's hair to comfort her. "Don't worry so, my child. Queen or not, we all love you, and you will always be Anu's beloved."

Inanna rests her head on her mother's shoulder. She smiles, while ambitious new schemes creep into her imagination. Then she frowns. *First, I must find a way to be with Anu. But how?* Her smile returns. *There must be a way. If I put my mind to it, I know I'll find it.* She sighs, nestling against her mother.

———

Inside the great palace at Larsa, Morgoth and his family sit around the huge council table considering what, if anything, they can do about Marduk.

Inanna rises, and bangs the table with her fist. "I demand Marduk's execution!" she says, in a wrathful appeal to Morgoth.

Morgoth appears amused. "Be sensible, Inanna," he says.

"Sensible!" She glowers at him. "Tell me, Father, what justice is there for me?"

Morgoth sighs. "You must wait," he says. "Wait for your grief to pass."

"Wait? How long?" she demands, her voice trembling with rage. "How can I wait while Marduk lives?" She launches a passionate tirade. "He fortified himself in Egypt, and now he defies anyone to bring him to justice. Yet you do nothing."

Morgoth frowns, growing impatient with her feverish demands. "I agree that Marduk has become a problem, but I don't have power over Eä or his family. Be content, I'll deal with Marduk in my own time." He turns away from her, ready to move on to someone else.

She grows defiant, refusing to be dismissed. "When is it *my* time?" she insists. "As Dumuzi's widow, I have a right to demand a life for a life. That's the law, isn't it?"

Utu rises. "Dumuzi's death was an accident, Inanna. There's no cause to demand Marduk's death," he says, attempting to reason with her. Instead, his defense of Marduk infuriates her more.

She turns on him in a rage. "No cause to demand his death? You left Dumuzi in Marduk's custody, didn't you?"

"That's what you asked me to do!" Utu argues, now furious at her attempt to blame him. "Marduk tried to protect Dumuzi, even after you urged Dumuzi to violate his own sister."

"It was Dumuzi's right!" she shouts. "He didn't deserve to die for it."

"True," Utu replies, "but Marduk didn't kill Dumuzi."

"Yes he did," she insists. "When Dumuzi died, he was acting on Marduk's orders."

"*You* were the one who begged me to hide Dumuzi. Have you forgotten? Marduk agreed only because he loved Dumuzi. He never wanted his brother dead." Utu takes a deep breath, and his voice grows calm. "This isn't a trial, Inanna. Let's wait until Marduk is here to defend himself."

"I don't need to wait for a trial!" she says, turning back to Morgoth. "As his widow, I demand justice right now," and she thumps the table again.

"Then I must grant your wish, Inanna," Morgoth says, stopping the argument. "Tell me, what punishment do you seek for Marduk?"

"The same fate as Dumuzi's," she says. "Death by Blaster."

A murmur of shock goes through the Council.

"Have you all gone mad?" Utu says to the Council. "I may support my sister in most things, but not in this. It isn't right. Dumuzi was only defending Eä's compound. He was simply doing what any loving son would do, what loyalty to his family demanded."

"Yes, to fight against us!" Inanna shouts, her face twisted by hatred. "If you refuse to shoot Marduk, then seal him in his pyramid like the dog that he is, and leave him to die!"

Sud gazes at Inanna, shaken by her daughter's cruelty. "You'd bury him alive?"

Before Inanna can answer, Utu shouts, "No!" in defiance of her gruesome proposal. "Vengeance is not worth war between our families. Do you think Marduk would be imprisoned willingly, or that Eä would allow it? Especially since Ninurta's men raided the compound illegally. *They* blasted Dumuzi."

Sitting in the back unnoticed, Ninurta smirks. *You might say we accomplished that mission with great success*, he muses.

Morgoth shakes his head and gives Utu an angry look of disapproval. Utu sits down.

"Marduk refused to give us his clones, didn't he?" Inanna argues back. "Traitors must die, even if it takes an army."

Morgoth quickly adds, "I agree. Laws must be obeyed." Inanna smiles, triumphant.

Utu jumps up again, anguish in his voice. "Don't listen to her, Father. Dumuzi's death twisted her mind," he says. "Yes, laws should be obeyed, but what kind of justice is this? You've sentenced Marduk to death without a trial! Without one word from him in his own defense."

"A travesty!" Sud says, supporting Utu. "How heartless of you, Morgoth. How could you take another son from Damkina, after she's had so much grief?"

"Enough!" Morgoth says, gazing at them in stern judgment. "Marduk must die."

A smile appears on Ninurta's face. *Just what Morgoth has been waiting for*, he reminds himself. *Eä and his son, both out of the way. The Fates are kind to us.*

———

When Utu comes to warn Marduk of Morgoth's decision to support Inanna's request, Marduk is puzzled. "Kill me? Why?" Marduk demands. *The bitch must be crazy!* he thinks to himself. To Utu he says, "Inanna urged Dumuzi to rape Geshtina. Dumuzi admitted it."

"I also believed Dumuzi," Utu agrees, "but Inanna will deny it. Even worse, she demands her widow's right to a life for a life."

Marduk grows suspicious. *There must be more to this than what appears*, he reasons. "I think Dumuzi's death is just an excuse to get rid of me. I have no doubt that Morgoth has heard the prophecy that I will rule Earth one day. With me dead, nothing can block his line to the throne. He'd rather kill me than risk..."

Utu hangs his head, looking ashamed and sad. "This is my fault. Dumuzi should have been tried for the rape immediately. Instead, I let you take him to the compound."

Marduk shouts, "No! Don't blame yourself. Blame Inanna!" Furious at Inanna's duplicity, he says, "She knew a son by Geshtina would secure her place as Dumuzi's queen. Don't you see? Dumuzi was just a pawn. Inanna and Morgoth are working together now."

"You don't have to convince me," Utu says, gazing at him. "My sister's ambition has no bounds. You should have seen her at the Council. She thirsts for your blood."

"So does Morgoth," Marduk says, "but none of this makes any sense. Morgoth knows I'd never kill my own brother!" *What else could be going on?* he wonders. *The*

*punishment for rape is solitary exile, not death. Exile was
Morgoth's punishment for raping Sud long ago.*

Recalling the chain of events, Utu is filled with sadness. "I'm sorry that trouble has come between our families again. We hoped Inanna's marriage to Dumuzi would
heal the old wounds, not this." Departing, Utu gives
Marduk a manly embrace, "You know, Morgoth ordered
me to help Inanna."

"You've been a good brother, Utu," he says, growing
serious. "My father refused to go against your father, but if
Inanna and Ninurta come for me, I must fight back."

Utu gazes at Marduk with deep concern. "Protect
yourself," Utu says.

Marduk gives him a sardonic smile. "When you see
Inanna, give her a message for me. Tell her, no one has the
power to change my destiny. Not even a queen."

———

The long-awaited starship from Arra carrying King Anu
and his entourage arrived on Earth for a brief visit. The
impatient crowd that had gathered to greet the King waited in the darkness for the descent of his shuttlecraft. This
great event had been anticipated for many shars, and now
it was actually happening.

A stately priestess, known by all as Nanche, wearing
crimson ceremonial robes, extends her arms skyward to
deliver an incantation for Anu's safe landing. Then she

gives the command, "Light the bonfires!" A horn blares. Seven bonfires rise into the night sky on the surrounding hills, lighting a clear path for Anu's shuttlecraft to follow.

Anu is met by an adoring crowd as he steps from the shuttlecraft. Morgoth rushes over to assist him. After a short speech to acknowledge his good wishes, Morgoth escorts Anu to a luxurious palace at Erech, one built especially for Anu a long time ago.

Because of the turmoil on Arra, Anu could not avoid the royal duties of his kingdom for long, but with Dumuzi's death and the delay of gold deliveries, a trip to Earth became mandatory. *What was going on between Morgoth and Eä?* Anu wondered. If Arra was to survive, it was up to him to set things straight. Now he had to deal with this quarrel over Marduk.

Since Anu's visit was limited, Morgoth scheduled Anu's royal tour to visit the most important places: the mines, the gold refinery, Eä's laboratory, the clone compound where Dumuzi died, and of course, Varda's clinic. Due to the animosity over Marduk, Varda volunteered to escort Anu to all the diplomatic meetings. As they travelled from place to place, she tried as best she could to explain the impasse between Morgoth and Eä. She told him that the storm seemed to center around Inanna now, and her insistence that Marduk be put to death.

At the end of the tour, Morgoth planned a farewell banquet for Anu, in preparation for his return to Arra. For days now, servants had been preparing a sumptuous evening feast to be held in the garden at Anu's lavish temple in Erech. Arriving for what they believed would be an outdoor celebration of peace, the families of Morgoth and Eä were escorted to a long banquet table lit by flaming torches.

As everyone watches, knowing how potentially explosive any situation might get with Morgoth and Eä sitting together, the tension in the air was palpable. Anu's presence seemed to be the only factor holding their tempers in check. It was going to be an interesting evening.

Reclining on plush couches covered with the softest animal fur, Anu and Antu appear ageless and unchanged. They drink wine from golden goblets while chatting with Morgoth and Eä, the earthbound patriarchs of Anu's royal descendants. Their sons Utu, Ninurta, and Lugal are also present at the table. Conspicuously absent are Marduk and dearly departed Dumuzi, although Dumuzi's ghost seems almost palpable, hovering, coloring every conversation.

The elder women sit together. Varda, Sud, and Damkina laugh and gossip, pretending nothing is wrong at all. Lugal's wife Ereshkigal, Ninurta's wife Bau, and Utu's wife Aya, chat together in a separate group, all uninvolved in the feud except for Ereshkigal, Inanna's sister, now Queen of the Kur. But Inanna is nowhere to be seen.

Anu looks up from his wine, and gazing around the room, suddenly asks, "Where is my sweet Inanna? Does she choose to offend me?"

The men around Anu grow silent, waiting for someone to answer.

Utu speaks up. "No, Poppy. She's still pouting over Marduk."

Spontaneous laughter from the men eases the tension.

Still chuckling, Anu says, "Is that all! Well, she's young. She'll get over it soon enough." When the humor passes, he sighs. "I should get back to Arra, but with all this discord over Marduk, I must stay until it's resolved."

Antu looks over at Anu. "Well, I'm glad we're staying," she says. "Arra doesn't feel like home anymore. The days are too hot and dry, and the skies so orange and dusty..."

While Antu complains, Morgoth rises and goes over to sit with Eä, out of earshot. "You're lucky Anu protects you, brother," he says. He emphasizes *brother*, a word he rarely uses since the division of territory at Larsa.

"Anu is fair and just, as usual," Eä replies, ignoring the suspicious epithet *brother*.

"Not this time," Morgoth says, his voice growing ominous. "Whoever helped Marduk escape will be banished, or worse. The act was treason."

Eä stays calm, unwilling to respond to Morgoth's attempts to enflame him. "Perhaps not," he replies, staying calm and detached. "Inanna's demands were outrageous. They were for murder, not justice, and Anu knows who encouraged her."

Morgoth glares at Eä. "Don't play games with me, Eä!" he says, raising his voice in anger. "You're not very good at it. When Anu finds out…"

A loud blast from a huge horn interrupts their argument and signals the beginning of the evening ceremony.

Nanche comes forward to invoke the required incantation. "Hear me, spirits of the heavens! Receive this fiery offering for each of Anu's line: for Morgoth of Sumer, for Eä of the Abzu, for Lugal of the Kur, and for Marduk who is banished from us."

For each name she speaks, she tosses a handful of sand-like crystals into an open fire pit. The crystals flare up into an explosion of rainbow colors.

"From this day forward," Nanche intones, "may there be peace in all the lands."

Morgoth rises. Standing beside Nanche, he proclaims. "We know that Marduk is in exile for his crimes against Inanna, but we hold no anger in our hearts for his family. We welcome Eä back to Sumer, and we forgive all those who helped in Marduk's escape."

While Anu and the group applaud Morgoth's speech, Ninurta scowls with anger. Without warning, he jumps to his feet, shouting, "Marduk escapes death, and traitors gloat. Since when does Morgoth forgive treason?"

Varda speaks up sharply. "Ninurta! Be silent! Sit down and agree with your father's peace terms."

Ninurta appears surprised by her harshness, but bows to her. "I honor your wishes, Lady." Ninurta sits down.

Anu says, "I want no more of this squabbling. I hereby pardon Marduk, as long as he remains in exile and causes no more trouble."

A murmur of surprise ripples through the group, but no one dares to protest Anu's command.

A group of young maidens rushes over to escort the Queen to her chambers. Antu announces, "This evening has exhausted me. If you excuse me, Anu, I will retire now to the House of the Golden Bed."

Anu smiles and waives his approval. No sooner did the maidens escort Antu away, than another group of semi-nude maidens, covered only in flimsy togas, approaches.

A dark-haired maiden says, "The Bed of Nighttime Pleasures awaits you, O Anu."

Giggling, a shy blonde maiden comes up to Anu. "The honored Sacred Maiden is waiting to pleasure you." She giggles, then bows low and runs away.

Anu beams at the news and prepares to leave. Suddenly, he stops, and turning back to the group, he says, "I almost forgot! Morgoth," glancing away at the maidens, "you and Eä," still glancing at them, "I want you two to divide Earth equitably among your sons."

Ninurta glares at Anu, offended by the command. "Does that include Marduk?" he asks.

Anu pauses a moment, distracted. "Well, no," he says.

Eä intercedes, "But Father, did you forget that you gave Babylon to Marduk?"

Anu chuckles at the maidens who smile and beckon to him. "Oh, so I did," he says. He looks back at Eä. "Very well, Babylon will remain Marduk's domain."

Anu glances over at the maidens again. Impatient, he says, "Just settle the rest among yourselves." Beaming with excited anticipation, Anu scurries off in delight, surrounded by the giggling young maidens.

———

Ever since Anu arrived, Inanna chose not to see him. By design, she waited for Anu to come to her. She was not a child any longer, but Anu would continue to treat her so. If she allowed it. She used the time to make careful plans: how to see him alone, how to gain his sympathy, how to get his promise to grant her wish. Now that he was actually on Earth, her one chance had come at last. At any moment, Anu would open the door and enter her chamber. She felt confident. *After all, he's just a male*, she told herself.

Entering, Anu sees Inanna sitting at her chamber window, gazing out at nothing in particular.

"You look so depressed, Inanna," he says. *This is not like my little Inanna*, he observes. *I thought she would run over and throw her arms around me, just as she used to.*

She glances over at him without a smile, and turns back to the window.

He comes over and sits beside her. "Grieving for Dumuzi?"

"No, Grandfather," she says, still staring out the window.

"Then what is it, my dear," he asks in a gentle voice.

"Destiny conspires against me." She heaves a sigh.

He chuckles. "No wonder you look depressed! You're too young and beautiful to be so angry at Destiny."

"The Fates took away all my hopes for the future." A tear trickles down her cheek.

'The future?" Anu chuckles again. "No one can know the future, my little one."

"Don't make fun of me," she snaps, turning to him in angry frustration. "I will be a queen, or the Aeons will hear my complaints all the way to Aaru! I swear it, by all the dark powers of Malkur."

"Dark powers of Malkur? Silly child," Anu joshes. "How can you expect to be a queen with Dumuzi dead? Without his son, you have no claim to his throne, or any throne."

"I know the law, Grandfather," she says, resolute. "My only recourse would be to marry someone else who could make me a queen. But the law says that when a man dies without a son, his widow can't marry a stranger, not if her dead spouse has brothers."

"Yes, that's true. The brother's duty is to marry her and have children by her, so that her husband's name shall not be blotted out. But Dumuzi's eldest brother is Marduk. Would you have a child by your husband's murderer?"

She jumps to her feet, furious. "By the stars, I would cut his throat first!"

"Then who?" Anu asks.

"I will go to the Kur," Inanna replies, "and claim my right to have a son by Lugal."

"Your sister's husband?" Anu stares at her in disbelief. "I fear she might kill you first, and then I would grieve for you the rest of my days. So no, I forbid it."

"Mother said you could make me a queen," Inanna says, "if you wished it."

Anu considers her proposal, not certain if she is serious. *I don't know what she's getting at, but anything else would be better than trying to seduce her sister's husband.* "I suppose I could," he says with caution, "but being a queen is a serious matter. It requires special knowledge. So even if I wished it, I'm afraid I couldn't." He hurries to ease her disappointment. "Besides, there are no kingdoms left to give."

He won't get off that easily, she thinks. "What about the Indus valley?" she asks.

He looks at her in surprise. *How does she know about that?* he wonders.

She smiles at him. "I could be a queen there, couldn't I?"

"That awful place?" Anu fidgets a bit, looking for some way out. Then he says, "The valley is nothing but mountains and wild animals. Hard even for natives. Worse for a queen."

"You exaggerate, Grandfather," she says. "It was like that here when we first arrived. All the land between the rivers in the north, all the Kur and the lands in the south. All were wild and mountainous. Now many people live there. The Indus valley could be beautiful, perhaps the most beautiful kingdom of all."

"Yes, I suppose that's possible, my dear," Anu says, still humoring her. "But it would take someone with great knowledge and skill to tame it. You have no training in rulership."

"What if I could get it?" she asks. "Everything I need to know is in the Codices, isn't it?" She waits for him to answer, but he sits pondering in silence. Urgently hoping to convince him, she says, "If I had them, would you make me Queen of the Indus then?"

"Of course, dear child," he says, "but the sacred knowledge in the Codices is vast. Without training, you would not even know what to learn." He shakes his head. "Even obtaining access to them is very unlikely. Very unlikely."

Undaunted by negativity, she presses him further. "But if I had them, you'd make me a queen then, wouldn't you?"

Great Sophia! Anu muses, *will she never give up?* He takes a deep breath, resigned to humor her for now. "Yes, I suppose I would, if you also understood their deeper meaning."

She smiles at him, sensing a victory. "If I did, then I could be a queen?"

Anu chuckles, if only to get her to stop. "How can I say no to you?" Yielding to her stubborn persistence, he says, "Yes, after all that, then you could be a queen."

"Promise?" she asks, pushing his limits.

Anu's mood changes. He grows stern, his voice harsh and commanding. "The first rule you must learn is to never question a king. A king's word is law."

"Yes, Poppy," she says, acting contrite. She beams at him, fully convinced that he will make her a queen, provided she can fulfill the requirements. *That will come later*, she assures herself, now content with having secured his promise.

"Ah, there's that beautiful smile," he says. "The long trip to Earth was worth it, my beloved child, if only to see you happy again.

She throws her arms around his neck and covers his cheeks with kisses, just as she did when she was little. He rocks with laughter and hugs her close.

————

Inanna sits before her chamber mirror and chatters with excitement. "This journey is my Destiny," she says. "I am certain of it."

Ninshubar stands over Inanna, grooming Inanna's long silky hair. "I am pleased you are so happy again, my lady," Ninshubar tells her, smiling.

"I'll get those Codices from Eä somehow," she says, aloud. "There must be a way."

Ninshubar's smile turns into a worried frown. She stops brushing Inanna's hair. "If you go on this journey to the Abzu, misfortune may befall you," Ninshubar warns.

"Stop your silly chatter and finish my hair," Inanna commands.

Ninshubar obeys.

"Eä is a man, isn't he?" Inanna asks.

Ninshubar considers her reply, then says, "Some men can be foolish over women who bring them pleasure, but dangerous when guarding their instruments of authority." Ninshubar brushes Inanna's hair vigorously, saying, "Eä holds great power."

"So do I," Inanna says, unwilling to hear anymore of Ninshubar's advice.

A long silence follows while Ninshubar goes on fixing Inanna's hair. With great care, she sweeps it up on top of Inanna's head, securing it with jeweled silver combs and a golden headband.

Inanna admires her finished hairdo in a mirror. She smiles into the mirror, the only reward Ninshubar will receive. Then she says, "Anu's sons growl like lions over a carcass, but they are too jealous of each other to notice a mouse steal away with a little piece of their meat."

Ninshubar appears frightened. "My lady, it is dangerous to tempt a lion in his lair."

"That may be true for someone as ordinary as yourself," Inanna says, turning to look at Ninshubar. Then she announces with a note of triumph, "Never forget, I am Anu's beloved."

Ninshubar remains silent. She goes to fetch Inanna's garments while listening to her mistress run on. Ninshubar returns with three different garments. She holds them up one at a time for Inanna's scrutiny.

Inanna considers each one, and then goes back to the first. "Not that one." She looks at the second one, then the third one. "No, too seductive. Save it for later," she says. Ninshubar holds up a fine linen sheath, almost pure white with gold trim. Inanna says, "That will do. Now bring the cloak and my favorite necklace." Ninshubar brings a cloak covered with white feather-like scallops and lined with cloth of azure blue.

Inanna slips into the sheath and waits while her servant adjusts it to her body. Then she adds golden bracelets that wrap around her upper arms like a serpent. Ninshubar wraps the exquisite azure-and-gold necklace of lapis lazuli about her neck and fastens it, then attaches golden earrings that match her headdress. As a final touch, she drapes the feathered cloak over Inanna's left shoulder, then stands back to wait for Inanna's approval.

"When I am Queen of the Indus," Inanna proclaims, "Morgoth will have to accept me to the Grand Council. At last, I will rule equally with the others. Think of it, Ninshubar! You will be personal slave to a queen."

Ninshubar bows to her, saying, "Yes, my lady. I will await your glorious return."

Inanna appraises herself in the mirror: perfect dress, perfect hair, and perfect makeup. She smiles with self-satisfaction, believing that it would be difficult for any man to resist a woman as beautiful as she is now.

———

Dressed in her carefully chosen ensemble, a vision softly alluring and elegantly tasteful in white, Inanna arrives for her visit to Eä's home in the Abzu. Despite her deceptively innocent appearance, Eä was on guard. He greeted her with suspicion.

"Why are you here?" he asks, making no effort to mask his distrust.

"What kind of welcome is that?" she asks, smiling at him seductively.

"What makes you think you're welcome?" he growls.

"I thought you'd be glad to see me," she says, pushing her way inside.

Eä steps aside and allows her to enter. "Glad?" he asks, his voice still stern. "After you demanded my son's execution? By the Aeons, I think not!"

She ignores his anger. "I bring important news, something I heard Morgoth say to my mother," she begins. She moves nearer, close enough for him to detect her exotic perfume. Now holding his full attention, she says, "He's planning to destroy the slaves... utterly."

Eä chuckles at her melodrama. *What kind of game is she playing this time?* he wonders. *I have no doubt Morgoth would be pleased to destroy the slaves, but he doesn't dare. Not as long as Arra is in danger. So why would she come all this way to bait me with such a flimsy story?* "Morgoth wouldn't do that, not if he ever wants to rule Arra."

"I tell you, he will," she insists. "He fears your creatures will mate with us one day, and he intends to put an end to it."

Eä considers the possibility that her message might be true. *Inanna must know that Varda produced a female prototype that can reproduce as we do*, he speculated. *After all, when Ninurta stole the clones and killed Dumuzi, what choice did we have?*

Without gold, the people on Arra were dying, and Anu had threatened to put Morgoth in charge of Earth. After that, the nurses rebelled and refused to be surrogate mothers. He had been delighted when Damkina volunteered to be a "birth goddess" for the female prototype, but then Damkina had died in childbirth. That was common knowledge.

When Dumuzi died, Inanna didn't realize that Morgoth's strategy to regain power had changed. He had tasted Arran blood, and now he would never be satisfied until there was more blood. Not the blood of the new crop of earthling slaves, but the blood of Eä and Marduk. Eä knew that Morgoth would not make his move until Arra was out of danger, because Morgoth needed Arra.

So there would be war. Morgoth pretended that his objective was virtuous, that he was opposed to inbreeding between the lofty visitors to Earth and the lowly slaves that they had created to serve them. His real objective was to prevent Eä from forming an army of earthlings that might be capable of actually defeating the Igigi. Morgoth also knew that Eä had no military training, so he was content to sit back and wait for Eä to solve the technical problems. But neither Morgoth nor Inanna knew that Marduk was not exactly "in exile." Eä had sent him to Arra, to the military academy. Marduk would return to train the earthlings to fight, and to kill. When the time came, Eä would be ready for Morgoth – with an army.

Eä smiles at Inanna again. "That's no surprise. He's been obsessed with virtue ever since he was exiled."

Inanna brightens. "Then that's the answer, isn't it? If Morgoth could stop the slaves from breeding with us, he might spare them."

"That's ridiculous," Eä says.

"What if I could persuade Morgoth to have the priests teach the slaves morality?" she suggests, hoping for a positive reaction.

"Morality!" Eä's voice booms at her. "Morgoth would just teach them fear. That's all he knows."

"Would you rather have them destroyed?"

Eä ponders the situation, and then shrugs with despair. "I doubt he'd ever agree to your plan. He's been determined to destroy them from the beginning."

"Won't you at least let me try?" She moves closer and grows seductive, toying with him. "I can come back," lightly touching his bare wrist with one finger, "and tell you what happened."

Her almost imperceptible touch sparks his interest, like a tiny static charge that passes between them, and his attraction is at once obvious. He gazes at her with a new intensity, saying, "By all means, if you persuade him to accept your plan, come back and let me know."

————

Inanna returns home to tell Morgoth the news. Now wearing her pilot's uniform and carrying her helmet, she finds Morgoth relaxing in his throne room. He is seated on a raised platform and resting against plump cushions atop a large couch. He fondles a sleek, full-grown leopard reclining at his side.

Standing before Morgoth, she says, "Eä knows what you plan to do."

"I don't care what Eä knows," Morgoth says before she can finish.

Undaunted, she climbs the steps to the pedestal and sits on one of the couches, taking care to sit on the far side of the leopard.

"You talk big, but it won't be easy to exterminate his slaves," she says.

"They multiply so fast, it takes all my time to deal with their issues. They're everywhere now." Morgoth grimaces. "But I'll be rid of them soon, you'll see."

"What about Anu?" she asks, looking at her father with childlike innocence. *Morgoth knows he can't possible meet his gold quotas without slaves.* "If the gold shipments stop, it would alarm him, wouldn't it?

Morgoth pauses to consider the merits of her argument. Then he says, "Arra has enough gold to survive for now, but you have a point."

"What if there was a way for both you and Eä to get what you want?" She watches his reaction.

His eyes narrow with suspicion. "What do you suggest?"

Inanna smiles. *He's taken the bait, and it was easier than I thought.* "I'll tell you," she says, tempting him, "but only if you promise to admit me to the Council after Anu makes me queen."

"Queen!" Morgoth bursts out laughing. "If that ever happens, my dear child, then you have my promise."

Inanna stifles her outrage. *One day you'll be sorry for laughing at me, you old reptile.* Instead, her eyes brighten and she smiles with delight. "Good. I believe Eä would agree to your establishing a priesthood. The priests would teach the slaves our ways, and they could condemn the noisy rutting that you hate so much."

Morgoth snorts derision. "That's not enough," he growls. "I don't want to interact with them at all!"

"What else do you want?" she asks.

"How can I ever withdraw from their affairs?" he grumbles. "Never, even if Eä's mindless apes could learn to live by laws that we enforce. Someone would always…"

Inanna interrupts his discourse. "Then that's your solution, isn't it?"

He gives her a puzzled look. "What do you mean, girl?"

"Kings!" she exclaims. "Let a few of the half-breeds who become endowed with some of our intelligence become kings. They will rule the slaves. Other half-breeds could become priests. As intermediaries, they would convey our instructions to the kings."

Morgoth pauses while he evaluates her plan.

She watches his reaction and sees that he is undecided.

"Consider this as the best part," she says, hoping to bait him with more benefits. "The priests can teach the slaves to worship us. We'd be gods! Think of that. It's simple, and you'd avoid all the aggravation and gain all the rewards."

"Worshipped as gods." Morgoth ponders her idea, turning it over in his mind like a new confection. "I like it," he admits, showing a faint smile. Then his face turns sour and his voice heavy. "Eä would never permit us to impose such restrictions on his creatures."

"Leave that to me," she urges. "All you have to do is remember your promise."

He gives her a derisive smile. "Of course, my little goose."

Despite his condescending tone, she is energized by his apparent willingness to collaborate in her plan.

As she rushes away, Morgoth calls after her. "Shall I welcome you back as queen, or as goddess?"

She turns back to him for a moment and stands with pride. "I will be queen!" She puts on her helmet and rushes out.

He gazes after her with amusement, stroking his leopard. Scratching the animal's chin, he waits for the big cat to lift his head. Gazing into those huge eyes, Morgoth says to the leopard, "Inanna can be such a foolish child."

———

The time came for Inanna to enact her plan to obtain the Codices, the last essential ingredient that she so desperately needed to become queen. She had arranged for the visit with Isimud, Eä's *sukkal*, a trusted emissary who took care of important details for Eä.

Isimud, a thin gray-haired man wearing a long robe, enters Eä's living area and bows to him. "Sire, the lady Inanna has arrived. She is waiting for you."

"Have you made all the arrangements? Food, wine…" Eä asks.

"Yes, Sire. Everything has been prepared, just as you instructed," Isimud replies. "I trust the lady will be pleased."

"Good," Eä says. "Show her in."

Eä moves to the far side of the room, intending to show indifference. He knew Inanna would not have come unless she wanted some favor from him. He did not trust her or the alliance she had promised to broker with his brother.

Inanna enters the room. She stands near the doorway, this time with a new image for Eä, one that had changed from the earlier innocent white to her present black ankle-length cape. The cape was ornamented with an intricate gold brocade woven into a tapestry depicting huge soaring eagles hunting for terrified deer. The brocade covers the shoulders, repeats along the hemline and up the opening, barely revealing the edges of a satiny gold lining. She wears no other jewelry except a simple band of gold across her forehead and over her lustrous black hair. Her makeup is perfect: luscious ruby lips, dark eye shadow, and black eyeliner with thick lashes that accent her almond-shaped eyes. She is stunning, every bit the image of a seductive goddess.

Eä stares at her, entranced.

She meets his eyes and holds him there.

He moves toward her, as if in a dream.

Without a word, she turns her back to him – and waits.

What does she want? he wonders. *Take her cape, idiot,"* he chides himself. Slowly, he lifts the cape from her shoulders. Her delicate fragrance swiftly envelopes him. *Jasmine… or honeysuckle?* he wonders. The aroma is so light and yet compelling that it confounds his brain.

As the cape slides away, his eyes are drawn to her bare back. Her black sheath is cut away to reveal her entire back, from neck to waist, down to the curve of her hips, and is held up only by shoulder straps. Her skin is smooth and golden. *Delicious*, he thinks, while his emotions savor every curve. He stands there, staring at her, until she turns to face him.

"Isimud!" he calls out, breaking the spell. Isimud appears, silent as a ghost. Eä hands him the cape. "Bring us wine, and food," Eä says. Isimud bows and vanishes.

While they wait for Isimud to return, Eä focuses once more on Inanna. The front of her dress is cut nearly to her waist, giving him just a glimpse of her full bosom. Her slender waist is encircled by an exotic gold chain, and the skirt opens with each subtle motion to reveal long and shapely legs. Above each elbow, she wears glistening armbands shaped like golden serpents. *She is exquisite*, he tells himself.

Isimud returns and spreads a table for a party-for-two. He covers the table with assorted delicacies: little cuts of roasted meat and fowl, bite-size fruits, dates, grapes, breads and cheese. Before he leaves them alone, he brings a tray of various wines and sets it beside them.

Eä beckons to Inanna to sit and partake of the feast he has provided for her. He pours wine and offers it to her, smiling with delight at her sensuous beauty. She moves beside him, and when they are both comfortable with their nearness, she holds out a morsel of his favorite sweet.

When he opens his mouth, she pulls back, teasing him several times while they both laugh. Finally, she puts the treat in his mouth. He savors it, exaggerating, but never taking his eyes from her face. Then she pours more wine for him, and each time he empties his glass, she refills it.

"You see?" she asks, noting that he is quite tipsy by now. "I told you Morgoth would agree to our plan." She moves to pour more wine.

He tries to stop her. "No, no. I've had too much already.

"Aren't you pleased with me?" she asks, pouting.

"I am more than pleased with you," he says.

"Don't spoil our party," she scolds. She pours the wine anyway. "How often do we celebrate such good news?" Then she stands over him, holding out the goblet.

He takes the goblet and puts it aside, then reaches for her.

She evades him, laughing. "Aren't you going to reward me? I did you a great service."

He gazes at her with desire, his animal appetite aroused. "Name it. It's yours."

Inanna pauses. *Be careful*, she thinks. *This may be my one chance.* "Let me see," she says, pretending to think about what she wants. "I know! Do you have the Codices?"

Drunk as he is, Eä frowns at her request. "Yes, but they are not mine to give. Ask me for something within my power."

Her delight turns to dismay. She turns away from him, pouting. "I've heard so much about them," she says. "Won't you at least show them to me?"

His smile and good humor returns. "For you, yes." He makes his way to a cabinet and opens it, revealing many stacks of trays, all neatly labelled. He turns to her, and with a flamboyant gesture, he says, "Behold! The supreme knowledge of the universe."

She breathes her astonishment at the glittering crystals. "Oh, how marvelous!" she gasps, hardly believing that she actually got him to reveal where they were hidden.

He pulls out a tray marked "Rulership." The velvet tray contains seven large crystals of different colors. He brings it to her.

She frowns. "How do you use them?" she asks. "They look like ordinary crystals."

"Not ordinary! When you activate them with a computer, they reveal the essential wisdom of each sacred function," he explains. He lifts out each crystal and shows it to her, one at a time. "This one's for 'Lordship,' this for 'Godship,' then 'The Exalted and Enduring Tiara,' 'The Throne of Kingship', 'The Exalted Scepter and Staff', 'The Exalted Shrine', and this beauty is for 'Righteous Rulership.'"

She takes the last one from him and examines it with wonder. "Are there more? Perhaps one for 'Queenship'?"

"Many more," Eä says. "The 'Functions and Attributes of a Fine Lady' gives a description of her royal temple and rituals. It describes all her priests, eunuchs, and maidens. Then there's one for 'Warfare and Weapons', another for 'Justice and Courts,' also 'Music and Arts.'"

By now, her eyes are wide with excitement.

Eä looks over at her, saying, "But this isn't any fun. I'm boring you." He takes the crystal and puts it back in the tray.

Inanna reaches out to stop him. "No! Tell me more. I want to know all about them."

Ignoring her demand, he gathers up the crystals and returns them to his cabinet.

She watches him in angry frustration. While he is at the cabinet, she opens an amulet on her waist chain, and with a quick motion, empties some powder into his goblet of wine.

When he comes back, he says, "Now, where were we?"

Her expression changes to a smile again. Adding some wine, she offers him the goblet. "How can I ever repay your generosity?" she asks, inviting him with her eyes.

He gulps down all the wine.

Still standing, she presses her body close to his face.

Aware of her exciting perfume and the promise of her body, he reaches out for her. He strokes her hips and thighs, and then moves his hands upward.

She smiles and pulls away, tantalizing him.

Now with his animal passion awakened, he pursues her.

She undulates over to a large couch. She stands there, removing her sheath in slow motion, tempting him with her naked breasts.

He lumbers toward her, heavy with the drugged drink, wanting her.

She waits, exciting him more with her titillating motions.

He takes her in his arms, caresses her shoulders and breasts with wonder.

She takes his face in her hands and brushes his lips with the hint of a kiss, a promise of fulfillment.

Wanting her beyond reason, he returns her invitation with a passionate kiss.

She surrenders, offering no resistance.

He lifts her onto the couch, breathing hard, ready to mount. He climbs beside her, and tears away the last of her undergarments. All at once, the drug overtakes him. He moans and collapses beside her.

Seeing him unconscious and in a drugged stupor, she pushes him away. She gets to her feet and stands over him, looking down with contempt. Then she retrieves her clothes, puts them on, and goes to the cabinet. Quickly, she selects the crystals she will need and rushes away.

Eä remains sprawled on the couch, unconscious.

————

The next day Eä wakens and looks around for Inanna. Finding her gone, he appears disappointed and calls out, "Isimud! Isimud! Where is Inanna?"

"Gone, Sire," Isimud says, appearing as silently as before. "She departed in her Warbird before dawn." Isimud gestures to the open cabinet. "I think she took something."

Eä jumps up. He rushes to the cabinet and stares in disbelief. *The sacred crystals! Great Goddess, forgive me!* He turns to Isimud in a rage. "How could you let this happen?"

"She said you gave them to her, Sire," Isimud stammers. "In return for, shall I say certain favors?"

Eä slams the cabinet doors shut. "How could I be so stupid?"

"You did get quite drunk last night, Sire."

Eä looks around, searching. "Where are my clothes?"

Isimud hands him fresh clothing.

Eä dresses in haste while Isimud watches. Then he rushes toward the exit.

Isimud calls after him, "Where are you going, my Prince?"

"To stop her," Eä calls, storming out without a backward glance.

Isimud stands, staring after him, wondering what to do.

———

Eä catches up with Inanna at Morgoth's palace. Circling in his Skybird, he sees her standing below, talking to her male copilot. He notices that she is now dressed in her pilot's uniform. *I may be too late*, he realizes. Ignoring the usual precautions, Eä brings his Skybird down right next to Inanna's Warbird just as she and her copilot prepare to leave.

Inanna shouts to her copilot. "Go! I'll distract him." The copilot nods and climbs aboard.

Eä races over to Inanna. "I want the crystals," he demands.

"No!" she says, resolute. "You gave them to me, don't you remember?"

"I wasn't *that* drunk," Eä says. "A thief and a liar isn't worthy of such sacred wisdom." He takes a menacing step toward her. "Give them back!" he demands.

Behind him, the Warbird lifts off with a roar and moves away.

Laughing at him, she says, "Try and get them now."

Standing in the downdraft of the engines, the wind whipping at his clothes, he turns to see the Warbird departing.

Still laughing, she says, "Boneless old fool!"

In a rage, he shouts, "Evil vixen!" Then he grabs her shoulders and shakes her violently. But she goes on laughing. He growls, "I should tear your throat out."

At once, she stops laughing. "Take your hands off me," she threatens, "or I'll have Morgoth roast you alive."

With a look of contempt, he shoves her away. Then he storms off toward the palace.

She calls out after him, gloating. "You'll never get them now!"

Chapter 6
QUEEN AT LAST

Eä strides into Morgoth's palace unannounced. Morgoth sits on his couch stroking his pet leopard. The huge black cat appears relaxed as it stretches out beside him.

"Your daughter stole the codices from me," Eä says, still angry. Demanding, he says, "I want them back!"

Morgoth smirks with amusement. "A lover's quarrel is none of my business."

Eä gazes at him, infuriated even more. "That's absurd! We're not lovers."

Noting Eä's strong protest, Morgoth reveals the slightest hint of a smile. Goading him more, he says, "From what I hear, that's not what you thought last night." Then he grows stern and accusing, "You colluded with her, didn't you?"

Eä pauses to consider. "Yes, I suppose I did," he admits, "but Inanna tricked us both."

"Speak for yourself," Morgoth says, his voice harsh. "I thought her plan had merits. In fact, I intend to lower kingship to Earth and put the priests in charge, just as she suggested."

"You can't," Eä shouts, protesting the decision. "That plan is an abomination!"

"Then why did you agree to go along with it?" Morgoth demands.

Eä pauses. He realizes he is trapped once more by Inanna's scheme. "Because it was the only alternative left."

"Precisely," Morgoth says.

"How can you cripple the destiny of these earthlings like that?" Eä asks.

Morgoth feigns a look of innocence at the question. "Destiny! What do I care about their destiny?"

Eä stares at Morgoth. *What's happened to him?* he wonders. *Has he lost all sense of compassion? I must reach him, find a way to convince him.* "Try to understand, Morgoth. These beings are sentient now. Someday they will be capable of autonomy, and freedom."

"I understand perfectly, but apparently you don't. Slaves have no autonomy, or freedom. I'm simply keeping my promise not to exterminate them, and I expect you to keep yours."

Eä stares at Morgoth, speechless. Feeling utter frustration, he storms out.

Triumphant, Morgoth watches him go, revealing only a scornful smirk.

———

With the stolen crystals now in her possession, Inanna rushes to a lavish feast given for Anu's departure at his temple in Erech. She can hardly wait to tell him that her plan has succeeded. She has secured the Codices, and now she can be Queen of the Indus.

The banquet hall is filled with guests who laugh and gossip while servants hurry about with huge trays of food and pitchers of wine and ale. Amid the festivities, Inanna sits beside Anu. Impatient to claim her reward, she waits until a servant fills all the goblets with more wine.

Offering a toast, Inanna says, "Let us drink to my success, great Anu. Now you can fulfill your promise."

Anu looks up at her with casual surprise. "Promise? What promise is that, my child?"

She puts down her goblet. "Don't you remember?" she asks, gazing at him in shock. "You promised me the Indus Valley if I obtained the sacred knowledge."

"Oh, that," Anu chuckles. *Dear me, what can I tell her? I must leave for Arra tomorrow. Look at her, eyes so hopeful. If I deny her the Indus, she will hate me. The last thing I need is to end this visit with tears and recriminations. Wait...* With a flash of insight, he knows just what to do. Taking her hand, he soothes her as he would a small child. "We were just playing a game, that's all," he says, "because you seemed so sad."

She gazes at him, stricken, but says nothing.

"I wish I could grant your heart's desire, my dearest, but you know it would only anger the others. We can't risk more animosity right now, can we?" Anu sips his wine and smiles at the festivities around him. *Now, there's an end to it*, he concludes.

Inanna rises. "With your permission, I will retire now," she says, choking back tears.

Anu nods.

Inanna rushes away.

Great Goddess, she pleads, her mind whirling, *what can I do now?* She stifles her fury as she wipes away impotent tears. *Think*, she rebukes herself, refusing to acknowledge defeat. *What would a queen do?* All of a sudden, she remembers what she learned from the Codices, *"To retain her power, a queen must never acknowledge defeat."* She smiles to herself. *Anu is just a male, isn't he? So I know exactly how a queen would secure her power. I'm not defeated yet!*

Laughing and joking with the others, Anu watches the entertainment, as if nothing important had just happened. To his surprise, when a group of giggling young maidens comes over to fetch him, he forgets the unpleasant incident with Inanna. He gazes at the semi-nude girls with delicious anticipation, wondering, *Which of these will it be?*

One girl speaks to him, hardly able to stop giggling. "The Chamber of Nighttime Pleasures is ready, Sire," she says.

Anu reaches out, but the girl turns away deftly. She joins the others. Beaming, Anu allows the playful maidens to escort him. Anu enters the Chamber, curious to know which special maiden was chosen to pleasure him on this last night. He goes to the bed and pulls aside the veils.

There, resting against plump pillows, Inanna waits for him on the bed. She is draped with love, feathered with temptation, a goddess of seduction and delight.

Startled by this vision, Anu stands motionless, uncertain.

Inanna takes command. She rises from the bed and comes near, enticing him with her perfume, tantalizing him with her bare breasts

He drinks the wine that clouds his mind, and when she leads him to the great bed, he no longer resists. Once in bed, he becomes aroused by her naked body and her sensual touch. Soon he surrenders to the moment and co-operates in the lovemaking.

Later, after their orgy of desire, Inanna cuddles beside him. She turns to him and strokes his lips with her finger, cooing to him softly, "Great Anu, will you still deny my wish?"

Anu puts his strong arms around her. "After your great gift to me, my beloved, how could I deny you anything?" he says.

Beaming, she whispers, "You mean… you'll keep your promise?"

"From this moment on, my dearest, you are Queen of the Indus Valley," he decrees. He strokes her face tenderly. "To consecrate this wondrous night, this temple will be your very own. It is my gift to you, for being Anu's Beloved."

"Oh, Poppy!" She squeals with delight and smothers his cheeks with kisses. Then she throws her arms around his neck and hugs him, just as she did when a child. As she looks over his shoulder, her smile fades, but her eyes gleam while visions of a glorious future as Queen of the Indus dance across her mind.

———

At Eä's palace in Eridu, Enki complains to Varda. Consumed by jealousy, he seems torn between love and hatred for Inanna.

"She's our father's mistress!" he complains.

"So?" Varda asks, smiling with amusement. "Why be jealous? He has so many."

"He disgusts me!" Eä spits out.

Varda gazes at him in dismay. "I've never seen you like this."

Eä paces in turmoil. "I feel crazed. I could kill her, but I burn with desire for her." He stops pacing and turns to Varda. "Now she's with him! My father, who happens to be the king!"

Varda gazes at him with a professional eye. "You're not a child, you know," she says. "After what you did, what did you expect?

"What do you mean?" He stands over her, glaring. "I did what I had to do."

"Stop it," she says, cutting him short. "You wanted her. For the first time in your life, someone got inside your skin and made you feel passion."

"If you mean hatred, you're right," he acknowledges. "She played me for a fool, and now she goads me with my father."

"Who are you angry with, Inanna or Anu?" she asks.

He sinks into a chair, glowering.

Varda approaches him and attempts to soften his humiliation with love. She puts her arms around him and strokes his head with tenderness. "She's just a child. What does she know of love? What we share is true and deep."

"Bah!" he says, pushing her away in anger. He walks off to distance himself, as if repulsed by her. "How could you understand? You're incapable of her passion."

She stares at him in disbelief, now injured to the core. "You're an ass." She turns away and slams out.

Alone in the empty room, he slumps into a chair, realizing how he must have hurt Varda. Feeling overcome with grief and frustration, he chastises himself. *This can't be*, he thinks. *Has that vixen cast a spell on me? I love Varda and I despise Inanna, and yet I long to be with Inanna. No, I must be going mad.* He pauses. *Stop it!* he commands, struggling to silence that terrible inner voice. Then he gazes at the door with sadness, thinking of Varda, and wonders what to do with these strange and contradictory feelings, so new and uncontrollable.

———

Inanna was eager to establish herself as Queen of the Indus Valley. She dressed in her aeronaut suit, summoned her Warbird, and flew up the great Indus River. When she reached the interior of the valley, she began searching for a perfect location for her palace. She considered the two largest cities. First Harappa, and then Kukkutarma, "the city of the cockerel," named for its practice of raising sacred birds. Both cities had thriving populations, but their palaces were unsuitable for a large royal household and had few comforts adequate for her own tastes.

She followed the Indus River back to the coastline, then south along the coast to the sacred city of Dwarka. A magnificent palace already existed there, and as she approached the beautiful edifice, she saw it sparkling in the sun. Crystal windows shone like mirrors, and the walls glittered with emeralds, sapphires, and rubies. The *jali*, delicately perforated lattices inlaid with geometric designs in silver and gold, cooled the arches and balconies along the exterior. Although the people of Dwarka could no longer remember exactly who built the palace, they now considered it a shrine to the "old gods" who once walked among them.

Inanna gazed at the palace. *Once she arrived with all the trappings of her royal retinue*, she reflected, *how easy it would be to convince them that she belonged to the old pantheon.*

Who but Eä could have built such a wondrous palace? Perhaps he built it to celebrate his love for Varda when they decided to raise the first two human children together. The Harappan civilization had flourished under their care. Later, their own child, Ningishzidda, was born. This son, who came to be known in Egypt as Thoth, was endowed with both Varda's medical knowledge and Eä's architectural abilities.

Why shouldn't I move into Eä's palace? she asked herself. After all, the place was perfect, and she was still Eä's kin, the widow of his true son Dumuzi. *I need no permission*, she thought, convincing herself. *Now that I am Queen, who would dare question my right to live there? Besides, it will be temporary, until I build my own palace on the Indus River.*

From her new home in Eä's palace, Inanna roamed her world to find the most powerful kings who governed the largest territories. She convinced them to let her train their daughters in the arts of seduction, skills that would make them valuable as wives to the sons of other kings. Since everyone knew, unskilled princesses were financial burdens more than assets, and because there were so many females, most kings agreed to send at least one royal daughter to Inanna. She created an area of her palace called the *Haram*, meaning forbidden. The young maidens she selected were housed there during their training, and guarded by powerful eunuchs.

Since the girls were so innocent and naïve when they arrived, Inanna predicted only a few would succeed. Those who did, would become the sophisticated envoys she planned to use to carry out her plans. It was essential that they remain virgins until they completed the training. The girls were expected to gain a personal awareness of the high value men placed on an untouched female. The maidens that survived the training would be virgins, but no longer naïve.

Nor would they be suitable for the unskilled males who rutted like barnyard animals. No, not these maidens. They were meant only for the young and inexperienced sons of kings. In turn, the maidens trained these young royals to be skillful lovers, males with the capability of pleasuring a woman. Marriage was always a possibility, but not an objective. Inanna knew that special young women who learned the subtle skills of tempting and controlling men with their creative repertoire of sexual enticements, would never be content being dominated by a crude and barbaric male. She began to imagine other plans for them.

When Inanna reached the stage of introducing her trainees to young princes, of secretly watching the couples in the throes of climax, she began to grow restless and irritable. Every time she watched a couple enjoy the pleasures of lovemaking, she was overcome with memories of her time with Dumuzi. He had been the last son of the "old gods" that had been eligible for marriage. Where would she find another like him?

While orchestrating all her grand plans to make herself a queen, she had overlooked one important step. A queen needs a consort. But not any consort. She needed a strong man who could lead an army, not a boy like Dumuzi. Her love for Dumuzi had been simple and sweet, but these days she longed for someone earthier, someone who could transport her to ecstasy. Did anyone like that exist on Earth? The only way to find out was to audition lovers herself.

———

In Inanna's bedchamber, a handsome young prince is making crude love to Inanna. Suddenly she grows angry and strikes him.

"Fool! Get away from me."

He stops fiddling and looks up in shock. "What did I do wrong?"

"You bumbling clod, you're unfit to share my bed, let alone rule as my consort king." She claps for her guards. "Is there no man who can end the emptiness in my heart left by my Lord Dumuzi?"

"Please, my lady." The young man kisses her feet. "Mercy, I beg you."

"Get away." Inanna kicks him. "You're a worthless piece of dung."

The guards come in.

"Seize him!" she commands.

The guards obey.

"Send him back to the fools who sent him," she orders.

The guards carry the struggling victim out.

Outside the bedchamber, the young trainees, the daughters of kings, watch in horror as the guards carry the young man past them.

"Another one," whispers one princess.

"Terrible," whispers another. "So many are sent to die after sharing her chamber of pleasures."

"You mean her chamber of horrors," comments an older girl, laughing.

Inanna emerges from her bedchamber. "How dare you criticize me," she scolds. "I am the goddess of love in this palace, and you are merely the mortal daughters of kings. Have you learned nothing from me? Didn't I train you not to waste your sacred lovemaking talents on those unworthy of our pleasures?"

The girls cower before her anger.

"Go to bed!" Inanna commands.

They obey immediately.

———

Sargon, a handsome new lover dressed in kingly robes, arrives in the city in a flurry of pageantry. High above the crowd, smiling and waving from his elephant's golden *houdah*, Sargon leads the flamboyant entourage to Inanna's palace. Following him are musicians, jugglers, dancers, and tumbling acrobats. Delighted onlookers cheer Sargon as he passes.

On the balcony of the Haram, all the excited young princesses peer down through the *jali* at the attractive stranger.

"Do you think he'll live to see morning?" one princess asks, smiling with sarcasm.

"He might. He's handsome enough to last two nights, maybe," another adds.

"Perhaps not. None of the others could please her," says a third.

"But just look at him!" one maiden says, pushing her way to the front. "I'll wager this ring that he wins her." She holds up a large golden ring studded with precious gems. They all begin chattering about him, betting on his mortality with golden bracelets and valuable trinkets.

"What would it be like to share his bed?" another princess asks, which sets off a new round of giggling and more speculation about his potential performance.

"Stop twittering like magpies," a solemn older woman commands. "Sargon is doomed like the rest." She removes her golden tiara as a final wager. "I wager he will not live until morning," she says, tossing the tiara on the doomed pile with the other stakes.

Without warning, the mood of the young women turns apprehensive. The laughter and betting ceases. Now they watch the jubilant procession below in silence, while sadness and concern for Sargon's life shows on each young face.

———

At Morgoth's palace at Larsa, Morgoth addresses the Council members who are seated around the table in order of their rank: his wife Sud, his brother Eä, his sons Ninurta, Utu, and Nannar. Last is Chief Medical Officer Varda. Between Ninurta and Utu, one chair is noticeably vacant – Inanna's chair.

"We have important new business to discuss," Morgoth says. I offer you Inanna's plan to lower kingship to Earth. If you approve, we'll begin selecting half-breeds to rule as kings over the slaves. This should save us all considerable aggravation.

Eä rises and addresses the assembly. "Inanna's plan does not deserve attention. We have a responsibility to show these loyal workers how to govern themselves and live in peace," Eä contends. "If we force kings upon them, our own history proves that kings will inevitably compete with one another for power. Eventually, they will teach these gentle beings to fight and kill. Such purposes are malicious, and not worthy of us."

Morgoth gazes around the table at stony faces. He turns to Eä, "We need to protect our genetic purity. To remain a superior race, we must withdraw from carnal affairs with these slaves. I intend to expel them from Sumer. Our only responsibility to these creatures is teaching them proper respect for our laws so they will know their place in this society."

Eä watches in dismay as Sud, Nannar, and Ninurta pound the table in support. Utu and Varda abstain.

A sudden noise at the side access interrupts the heated discussion. All eyes turn to the doorway as Inanna makes her entrance. She is spectacular in her queenly regalia. While everyone watches in astonishment, she takes the empty seat at the table.

When Inanna is settled, Morgoth says, "Let me officially welcome Queen Inanna to our Council. We bestow upon her all the rights and privileges due her as Queen of the Indus.

Inanna nods to Morgoth, and smiles.

Eä glares at her.

Morgoth continues, "As I was saying, we need priests to steer the growing masses away from their vulgar ways. If they are capable of learning to worship us as gods, they will fear our power, and we should be able to control them."

"That's ridiculous!" Eä declares. "If we set ourselves up as gods, we will soon be struggling against each other for allegiance of their growing tribes. It will destroy our harmony and set family against family, brother against brother. Is that what you want?"

Growing angry, Nannar, Ninurta, and Utu all rise to speak at the same time.

Morgoth points to Ninurta, "First we'll hear from Ninurta, then Nannar and Utu."

Ninurta's voice rings out, loud and clear. "There are too many slaves, and their numbers are growing as we speak. Soon it will be too late to bend them to our will. Someone must teach them to fear and respect us."

Nannar rises, saying, "I agree with Ninurta. Get them out of Sumer and the sooner the better. Let them rut like the animals they are, but in the wilderness – where they came from."

"Hypocrites!" Utu shouts. "Admit the truth, both of you, that what you crave most is to be worshipped as gods. All you crave is power."

Ninurta remains seated. Smirking, he says, "Without power over the slaves, they'll soon infest the whole planet. Do you want to be overrun by an inferior race?"

Utu glares back at him, "Desire for power only hides your weakness."

Morgoth pounds his gavel, "Order! Order! Stop the bickering. Let's settle this matter."

The group grows silent. Utu and Ninurta glare at one another.

Inanna rises to speak, commanding the attention of all those present. "Might I remind the noble Eä that he agreed to this plan? Although it may be a compromise at best," she says, smiling at him seductively, "it is better than exterminating his creatures." She turns to the group, every inch a queen. "I say it is far better to be worshipped as gods, and let the kings pretend to rule."

Eä frowns at Inanna, smoldering inside. He remembered putting his hands around her throat. *I should have squeezed the life out of her then – while I had the chance.*

Morgoth's supporters pound the table in agreement.

"Very well," Morgoth says. "All those in favor of lowering kingship to Earth."

Sud, Nannar, Inanna, and Ninurta all raise their hand. Eä, Utu, and Varda abstain.

"The matter is settled then," Morgoth says. He bangs his gavel. "So be it."

Chapter 7
SARGON'S DOOM

That night Sargon enters Inanna's bedchamber with great command. She gazes at him with bewitching eyes, enticing him to share another of her infamous nights of love. Her sheer gown of pale yellow, with a fragile web of tiny pearls and jewels that allows only a tantalizing glimpse of her full breasts and hips, is perfection. Her long dark hair cascades down her back and covers her shoulders.

He stands near the entrance, unmoving, as if entranced by the vision of her.

She gestures toward a small table where two crystal goblets stand beside a carafe of wine.

He goes to the table and holds up a goblet, silently inquiring if she wants some.

She nods. While he pours the wine, she slithers toward him, still without a word. She comes closer, exciting him.

The air around him fills with subtle scents of vanilla and cinnamon, and perhaps a subtle hint of jasmine. She is deliciously tempting.

He holds out a goblet of the wine, drawing her closer.

She moves toward him, undulating, smiling, eyes smoldering with seduction, pleased that he is already doing her bidding. She reaches for the wine, still smiling at him.

Just as her fingers are about to touch the glass, he pulls it away.

Her smile fades, and her expression turns to shocked surprise.

He waits.

She pauses, uncertain. *Does this impudent male dare to tease me?* Testing him, she moves closer and reaches for the wine again.

He smiles graciously, but when she grasps the goblet, he does not release it.

Indignant, she attempts to pull it from his grasp, but he pulls the goblet firmly against his chest. Then he brings his other arm around her back and jerks her to him.

Now she is angry and tries to push him away, but he is too strong.

She opens her mouth to call out to her guards.

"Have some wine, my lady," he says, and putting the goblet to her lips, he fills her mouth with wine.

She swallows and sputters, choking, gasping for air.

When she removes her hand from the goblet, he quickly downs the remaining wine and tosses the goblet, still holding her firmly to him.

Recovering, she begins to struggle again, but he grasps her flailing wrist and holds her in his arms, helpless.

Once more, she opens her mouth to call out, but he quickly releases her wrist and covers her mouth with his huge hand to stifle her. "Be silent, my lady," he commands her in a hoarse whisper. "I know all your tricks, so I will not be a meal for your lions tonight."

Eyes wide with surprise, she stops struggling.

"I warn you, do not cry out," he commands.

She nods.

He removes his hand from her mouth. "That's better," he says, lifting her into his arms. He carries her to the bed and throws her down into the huge pillows.

She stares, watching as he removes his robe, fascinated by his broad chest and muscled arms. "Well? What are you waiting for?" she asks.

In no hurry, he moves beside her on the bed. Stroking the inside of her thighs, while he covers the side of her neck with small kisses.

Overcome by so much stimulation, she tenses and tries to push him away. "Get away from me, you pig!" she mutters. When he doesn't obey her command, she sinks her long nails into his chest, drawing blood.

He ignores the pain. Continuing to kiss her neck, he moves his hands up the inside of her thighs to the sacred mound between her legs.

Like a thunderbolt, she strikes him a mighty blow on the face. "Get off me!" she orders in a hoarse whisper.

He rises up on his knees, straddling her, holding her down between his legs.

Once more, she attempts to call out to her guards.

He lowers his body and stifles her call with his kiss.

She struggles under him like a wildcat, kicking and clawing for some way to hurt him. Unable to reach his genitals, she bites his lip, drawing blood again.

"Wildcat!" he mutters, and strikes her hard. "You don't want to be loved, you want to be conquered. So be it," he says, ripping away her fragile dress.

Now naked before him, she continues to struggle, refusing to submit.

Holding her arms, he wrestles with her until she grows weary.

She grows still, breathing hard, exhausted.

Then he lowers his body onto hers, penetrating her, slowly moving inside her.

She moans, relaxing, moving with him. At last, she surrenders to him in a crowning release of great passion. Then, rocked with huge sobs, her tears flow, as if freed at last from a deep well of pain.

He holds her, cradling her, comforting her like a child until her grief passes.

———

The next morning Sargon appears with Inanna on the balcony of the palace. The crowd cheers their approval of Sargon, the first candidate to survive a night with Inanna. Both smiling and joyful, Inanna announces that Sargon will be her consort, and their king.

Soon Inanna makes known her plans to leave Dwarka and build a new palace in the Indus Valley. The new palace, even more magnificent than the one at Dwarka, will be built in Kukkutarma, "the city of the cockerel." Later, Inanna and Sargon would change the name of the city to Agade, the "gateway to Paradise."

After many moons, the beautiful palace in the city of Agade is completed. Inanna has been very happy with Sargon, and now it brings her greater joy to offer him a brand new royal residence from which he will rule, a lasting token of her love for him.

Lugal waits for a reasonable passage of a time before coming to Agade to meet Sargon. For appearances, he comes to wish them well. However, in the darker recesses of his mind, he cannot resist poisoning their future dreams. Finding himself alone with Sargon, he takes advantage of Inanna's absence.

"I must compliment you on the beautiful palace you have built," Lugal says. "Such beauty will be a lasting tribute to your love for Inanna."

Sargon beams. "A small reflection of Inanna's great beauty."

"True, true." Lugal frowns, appearing sad. He sighs. "Too bad your city can't be consecrated like the others."

Sargon is puzzled. "Like the others?" he asks. "What do you mean?"

Lugal smiles. "The other gods in the royal family," he says, "but of course, they will never allow it."

"Why not?" Sargon asks.

"Because you are mortal," Lugal says, watching Sargon's reaction.

"What difference does that make?" Sargon argues. "Inanna is divine, and she has made me her consort to rule with her, as an equal."

Now Lugal spies the opportunity to plant his poison seed. "Inanna's divinity is given, but your kingship is not. No doubt, it will be questioned." He pauses, waiting for his message to sink in. "Of course, there are ways to protect yourself."

"Protect myself?" Sargon looks genuinely troubled. "From what?"

"From having anyone question your right to be king," Lugal says. "If Agade is to be a capital city, it must be consecrated, just as Marduk's city of Babylon was."

"I don't understand," Sargon says. "How is Agade to be consecrated?"

Lugal chuckles. "I keep forgetting that you have not been instructed in our divine protocol." He sits down, gesturing for Sargon to take a seat near him. "Do you know how Babylon was consecrated?"

Sargon shakes his head. "I have never heard about it."

"An oracle, a priestess with special ability to foresee the future, places a sacred sword on hallowed ground within the city," Lugal says. "So you see, a capital city is twice protected, by both sacred ground and sacred sword."

"So what should I do, call the Oracle?" Sargon asks.

"No," Lugal says. "She can't come to Agade unless she is commanded by the gods."

"Then what is there to do?" Sargon asks.

Lugal pauses, making him wait for the answer. "Now listen carefully. By removing the sacred sword and some of the consecrated soil from Babylon, and then implanting it in Agade, you can consecrate your own capital city and make it sacred."

Sargon just stares at him a long time, astonished. "Steal Marduk's sword?" He shakes his head. "I can't do that. Inanna would never allow it."

Lugal smiles. "Inanna doesn't have to know, does she? Just keep it a secret from her."

Sargon considers the suggestion, but still he shakes his head. "If Marduk found out, he would punish me."

"How could Marduk ever find out?" Lugal asks. "No one knows where he is, and he's certainly not in Babylon, so who will know?"

Sargon considers Lugal's argument, but still appears unconvinced.

Lugal continues, hoping to convince him. "How else will you legitimize your kingship? If you want to reign beside Inanna as her equal, you must validate your right to rulership. Inanna may balk if she knew, but once you succeed, she will be proud of your courage."

"Then it must be done!" Sargon says, bright with renewed enthusiasm.

"Good man," Lugal says, "I knew you'd understand."

Lugal pours wine for them both and offers a toast to Sargon's success. They drink to seal the bargain.

———

With his business in Agade finished, Lugal returns to the Kur. When Ereshkigal comes to greet him, he can hardly wait to tell her the news.

"So you're back," Ereshkigal says. "How goes it with my sister Inanna?"

Lugal smiles at her with elation. "You won't believe this, but her stupid husband agreed to steal the sacred sword from Babylon!"

"What?" She gazes at him with disbelief. "He wouldn't dare."

"Oh, but he will," Lugal reassures her.

She scoffs. "Inanna will stop him."

"That's the beauty of it," Lugal brags. "He won't tell her until the deed is done. Isn't that priceless?"

She frowns. "What did you tell him?"

Grinning, he says, "Only that if he removed the sword from Babylon and replanted it at Agade, his power would then be as divine as Inanna's."

"You lied."

"Of course." He shrugs and goes to his throne.

Ereshkigal watches until he sits. Then she says, "You know very well that Inanna might make him king, but Sargon will always be mortal."

"But he doesn't know that, now does he?" Lugal says. "We know his power will never equal hers, no matter how many sacred swords he may plant in Agade."

Still doubting how Sargon could have agreed, she asks, "Did you tell him that if he defiles the sacred sword, Marduk will go after him?"

"That's the whole idea, isn't it?" he argues. "Wherever Marduk is, he must be eager to return from exile. Now he will have a reason."

She goes to sit beside him on her throne. "How clever you are, Lugal. Once we know Marduk is not in the Abzu, we can establish our supremacy over the entire continent."

"Exactly," he says, giving her hand a reassuring squeeze. "We shouldn't tempt the Fates by rejoicing, my dear, even if we are certain that Sargon's pride will ruin him."

"You're so right," she adds, with a scornful snicker, "and perhaps ruin my little sister as well."

———

Returning to Agade from a brief trip to Harappa, Inanna is surprised to see a celebration in the palace garden. Amidst music and feasting, Sargon is talking with a group of strangers from outside the palace. When Inanna arrives, everyone turns to look at her. They smile, as if she is the guest of honor at her own party.

Sargon goes to her. "Come, my beloved," he says, beaming at her with excitement. "I have a surprise for you." He takes her hand and leads her to a remote corner of the garden.

Once there she is puzzled to see some type of excavation that has been covered with a ground cloth. *Who's been digging in the garden?* she wonders. She looks around, growing even more suspicious. *Why are all these people here?*

"What is it?" she asks.

"Look," he says, pulling aside the ground cloth. "This is what Agade is celebrating."

There in the pit she sees the jeweled hilt of a large sword buried in the ground. She gasps. *It can't be!* she tells herself. "What have you done?" she says, almost afraid to ask.

"This is the sacred sword, the one from Babylon." He turns to her, standing proud and strong. "I planted it here in our garden with its consecrated soil."

You fool! she screams to herself. *You utter fool.*

"Now Agade will be a center of power, just like Babylon," he announces for all to hear.

Inanna glares at him. "Who told you that?" she demands.

"Lugal," he says. Recognizing her angry scowl, his smile fades.

"Lugal!" she cries. "If you believed him, then you're a dupe." Her anger grows. "You should have asked me before committing such folly," she scolds, "unless our love has been corrupted by your arrogance... or your ambition to power."

He stares at her with shock and disbelief. "How can you say that? I only wanted you to be proud of me."

She softens, showing concern for him. "Don't you realize what Lugal has done to you?" She searches his face for some glimmering of understanding. "No one, not even the gods, would dare to move a sacred sword without Morgoth's command."

Sargon looks at her, bewildered. "Lugal said my kingship would never be legitimate without the sword."

She says, "I made it legitimate when you became my consort, but now you are Lugal's fool. Bait for Marduk. Do you think the gods will let a mortal defy their authority?"

He stands before her, still not comprehending the gravity of what he has done. Despite what she has said, he tries to justify his crime. "Lugal said that this would be the only way I could stand beside you in divinity."

She laughs, but her laughter is bitter. "You think the sword made you one of us?" She gazes at him with sadness and touches his face with love. "Oh my beloved, you'll learn soon enough that you are not divine. No one can protect you now."

———

News reaches Marduk in Egypt where he is training his army. When he hears of Sargon's violation of his sacred city of Babylon, Marduk grows furious. At a deeper level, he recognizes that he and Inanna are truly vicious enemies. She accused him of murdering Dumuzi, demanded his death, forced him into exile, and the score was left unsettled.

Now everything has changed, he tells himself, while various notions of reprisal spin wildly in his head. *Sargon must pay for what he has done*, he vows. How can he obey Anu's edict and remain in exile after this? *I must reassert myself, return to Babylon*, he broods. *The defilement of my city must be a sign. My Destiny time is here at last.*

In his mind, Marduk dreams of driving Sargon to madness, even to death. He envisions inciting rebellions against Sargon that inflict agitation, days and nights without sleep, which in all probability would lead to death. *After Babylon is restored, it will be time for me to claim my rightful power and rule this land. That is my Destiny.*

———

Older and stronger now, Marduk brings his great army from Egypt and prepares to enter Babylon. His palace looms in the distance. He stops to gaze at his city. Once he enters Babylon, the conditions of his exile would end. The death sentence that Anu had lifted from him, only while he remained in exile, would be restored. He would have to fight Morgoth, or die.

An officer, who is also a friend, rides his horse up beside Marduk. "There it is, Babylon," he says.

Marduk holds back his restless stallion. "We've been away a long time."

"Are you sure?" his friend asks. "Once we go in, you know what it means."

Marduk scoffs at him, impatient with indecision. "I didn't bring an army to the gates of my city only to go back to Egypt and cower in exile. Babylon will be restored, and then Sargon will pay for defiling my sacred ground."

Marduk signals the advance.

When the army reaches the palace, Marduk and his officers march inside. The palace is empty. Everything is covered with dust. Marduk climbs to his throne and sits down on the dusty seat. "I'm back," he says, looking every bit a king.

His smiling officers salute him, shouting "Hail Marduk, King of Babylon!" Deep down they all know the truth. From this point on, they will all have to fight to stay alive.

Marduk beckons to his friend. "Send this message to Morgoth, and make sure he knows it's from me," Marduk commands. "Tell him that the sacred sword of Babylon will not remain at Agade. The rebels who profaned my city will be punished."

Marduk's friend looks at him with concern. "Morgoth will come for you," he says.

"Then let him come," Marduk says. "Send it!"

His friend salutes and leaves.

Marduk gathers his other officers into a group and shows them a large map of Agade. *Now we'll teach that bitch goddess's arrogant little hare a lesson. Inanna will rue the day she sent a mortal to steal what is sacred from me*, he muses.

Pointing to several locations on the map, Marduk gives his men instructions, "First, I want each of you to position some of your men strategically at these key places. Then we'll surround the city."

"What happens after that?" one officer asks.

"The fun begins," Marduk says. "We'll instigate rebellions inside Agade such as Sargon has never seen. Our attacks will come at random during the night, from all sides, so that he'll never find rest. We'll vex Sargon until he wishes he were dead."

"What about the sword?" asks another officer. "Do you know where it is?"

"No, but it shouldn't be hard to find someone who'll tell us," Marduk says.

"With a little help," one man adds, and the rest of them laugh. They all knew how to get information when needed.

When the laughter fades, Marduk gazes at the eager faces of his men. "So, are you with me?"

They all raise their fists. "To Agade!" they cheer in support.

———

Thundering into Agade with flaming torches, soldiers carrying Marduk's banner set fire to homes and fields of wheat. As invaders drive away sheep and destroy food stores, leaving the city to starve, people watch in terror. In desperation, the people of Agade demolish statues of Inanna and Sargon, hoping to appease Marduk's invading soldiers. Then they drive Sargon's priests from Agade's temple with stones. While the city burns, they erect statues of their new god, Marduk. Many fall to their knees in worship, pleading with Marduk's statue to spare them.

Inside Inanna's palace, Sargon appears gray and weary. "My dearest Inanna," he confesses, "how I long for peace and the happy life we once knew."

The youthful Inanna, ageless, tries to encourage him. "Try to rest, my dearest," she says. "These attacks can't last much longer."

"How can I rest?" he complains. "Every time I close my eyes, another attack seems to come out of nowhere."

Exhausted, he sits up with great difficulty. "Our armies are fearful and growing rebellious. I'm so tired. If only you could help me," he says, grasping her hands and pleading to her with bloodshot eyes.

"I can't," she says, pulling away. "You know I am one of the lawmakers. If I am partial to you, it would start a major war!"

He falls back onto his pillows, covering his burning eyes with both hands. "I know all this is my fault. I never should have defiled Babylon." He removes his hands and looks up at her, tears streaming from his eyes. "Help me, Inanna. Can't you see? Marduk is killing me!"

She looks at him with pity. "I know you are tired, but somehow, you must find the courage to carry on alone. If I move against Marduk now, the gods would unite against us both. They *will* destroy us."

Looking wearier than ever, he sighs. "I'll try to rest," he says.

Hoping to comfort him, she strokes his brow.

He closes his eyes and relaxes. Just as his breathing becomes regular, the alarm sounds another attack. Startled, he jumps up and grabs his armor in a rush to answer it.

"No!" Inanna protests. "You must rest."

"I can't," he argues. "You know I can't," he says, struggling with his armor. Suddenly, he grabs his chest and collapses in agony.

Inanna rushes to him, but she sees he is ashen and can't breathe. She tries to comfort him. "Don't leave me, my beloved," she begs, hoping to call him back to life. Gripped by excruciating pain, he does not hear her. With his last agonizing breath, he dies in her arms.

Chapter 8
LUGAL'S TREACHERY

When Morgoth hears that Marduk had come out of exile and reclaimed Babylon, he calls the only available Council members to an urgent meeting at his palace in Larsa. Morgoth gazes around at their faces, only six present beside himself: his wife Sud, his sons Ninurta, Utu, Nannar, his security officer Varda, and Eä's faithless son Lugal. *Not much to choose from*, he reflects.

"Now that Sargon is dead," he begins, "the matter of the sacred sword is still unsettled." He pauses, waiting for a reaction. "I need a volunteer, someone to drive Marduk off the throne in Babylon." Everyone is silent. "Have you all become cowards?" he asks, still waiting, but still no one speaks up. "We all know Marduk is a difficult problem. With his well-trained army now in Babylon, we must get him back into exile without provoking him."

Lugal rises. "I'm certain that any plan to force Marduk to leave Babylon will fail," he argues.

Morgoth glowers at Lugal. "Why?" he demands.

"He's too strong," Lugal replies. "Marduk has no reason to leave now, and if he returns to Egypt, he'll just grow stronger."

"Then find a reason!" Morgoth commands, loud enough to make the whole room shake.

"Me?" Lugal appears flustered. "I'm his brother," he says, trying to weasel out. "He'd never listen to me."

"As his brother, you're the best one for the job," Morgoth insists.

Ninurta, Utu, and Nannar pound the table in agreement, smiling, relieved to have escaped such an unwelcome mission.

Morgoth frowns at them. He turns back to Lugal. "Marduk must leave Babylon immediately, and take his men with him."

"Or what?" Lugal asks.

Morgoth pauses. His eyes narrow. "Or he will die," Morgoth snarls.

A chill settles upon the room. No one dares question Morgoth's decree, or even think the unthinkable. What will happen if Marduk refuses to leave?

Lugal turns to Varda for support, but Varda looks away, remaining silent. *Lugal, what trouble have you brought us now?* she wonders.

Lugal sighs. "Very well," he says at last. "I'll abide by the Council's decision.

"Good," Morgoth says, nodding his approval.

————

Before meeting with Marduk in Babylon, Lugal goes to Agade to seek an alliance with the petulant Inanna, still mourning her dead consort.

"My Lady Queen," he opens with eloquence, bowing low to show respect for her. *Nothing softens a woman's injured pride more than deference*, he tells himself, noting her tiniest smile in response.

"What brings you to Agade?" she asks in a cordial tone.

"Morgoth sent me to persuade Marduk to step down from his throne in Babylon and return to exile," he explains.

Instantly, her smile disappears. "Don't speak to me of Marduk," she snarls, "unless you tell me he's dead." She glares with hatred. "Marduk killed Dumuzi, and now Sargon. I curse him with every breath I take!"

"I curse him, too," Lugal agrees, attempting to match her outrage. "It wasn't enough that Eä gave him authority in Egypt. If Marduk returns with his army now, he'll seize all of my lands in the Kur and usurp my throne as well."

"Why come to me about that?" she demands, scoffing with contempt at what seemed to her only a petty complaint. "When Dumuzi died, you lifted no hand to fulfill your duty to me."

He looks down, *Think fast*, he warns himself, *or your goose will be cooked to a crisp*. Lugal gazes at her with sad, remorseful eyes. "I would have welcomed you to my bed, lady, but I could not dishonor my wife to intercede against a sister's wrath." He reaches out for her hand.

Inanna jerks her hand away before he can touch her. *Dishonor Ereshkigal?* She thinks, rage growing inside her. She gazes at him with venom. *Indeed! What about the dishonor to me?* She looks away, dismissing him with disdain.

Undaunted, he presses forward. "We have a common enemy, my Lady." He pauses to judge the effect of his new words. "One that grows stronger every day." He waits until he regains her interest. When their eyes meet, he says, "You can be certain, Marduk will come for your lands soon enough."

Blazing with fury, she shouts, "Let him try! I will move against him with all my armies and drive him out of the Indus."

"As would I," he says, "but I suggest a more subtle strategy."

"Why?" she demands. "I thought you wanted him dead."

"To that end, we agree," he says, sweet-talking her. "But I'm bound by Morgoth's command. You know it's one thing to get Marduk to leave Babylon with his army, but quite another to get him to agree to go back into exile.

"That's *your* problem, isn't it?" She considers the situation, and then asks, "What do you expect *me* to do about it."

"Nothing, for now," he says, "but the time may soon come when you will need to make a stand against him in battle. Be prepared, that's all."

She turns to him in surprise. "So you plan to fight Marduk?"

"No," he says. "I plan to destroy him."

———

The meeting between Marduk and Lugal took place at the *Esagil*, which means "a house whose head is lofty." This was the famous "tower" of ancient Babylon. So much resentment had built up between the two brothers that Lugal did not know if he could ever reach any agreement with Marduk. The task before him seemed formidable.

Marduk was already angry. "You call yourselves gods," he scolded, "and yet you let the kings and priests corrupt the cities. They were supposed to maintain basic services, but when I returned, the city had no lights or running water. I had to rebuild everything."

"And so you have," said Lugal, "especially the waterworks." Lugal chose his next words carefully. "Ordinarily, you would be commended, but crowning yourself king in Babylon has blackened your name. When you returned from exile, you broke your promise to Anu and defiled his law."

Marduk blazes with anger at Lugal's criticism. "Who are you to speak to me of broken promises?" he whips back. "It is you who defiled Anu's law. While I was away, you stole the royal symbols of my kingship that Anu bestowed upon me."

Lugal protests his innocence. "You offend me, brother," he says, feigning astonishment. "I merely wanted to keep them safe until your return from exile. Your royal scepter and the radiating stone are in the Kur."

"In the Kur!" Marduk exclaims. "Then get them."

"I can't go now," Lugal claims. "You'll have make the trip yourself if you want them."

Marduk glares at him, furious. "You know I can't leave. If I do, the water won't flow and the lights will go out again. Without lights, the city will return to darkness and confusion, and without water, sickness will spread."

Lugal puts his hand on Marduk's shoulder, smiling. "You needn't worry," he says, his voice gentle. "If you leave, I'll see that nothing disturbs the order of your city."

Hearing Lugal's offer, Marduk gazes at him. Suspicious and uncertain, he turns away.

Lugal pursues him, faking sincerity. "We're brothers, aren't we? Go ahead. I'll take care of everything."

"Are you sure?" Marduk asks. "I must have the radiating stone to finish the repairs."

"You have my solemn promise," Lugal says.

"See to it, then," Marduk says. "I'll hold you to your word.

Chapter 9
ATTACK ON BABYLON

Reaching Babylon at night, Lugal and his men enter Marduk's empty palace with caution. Lugal leads the way from room to room, making sure no one is there.

"He's gone," Lugal says. "Follow me."

He leads his men deep into Marduk's mysterious underground chamber. There they walk across a long catwalk high above the deafening roar of machines pumping tons of water into the city. At the end of the catwalk, they find a heavy door with a sign warning, "Restricted Area. Keep Out."

Ignoring the warning, Lugal opens the door. Inside the room, he sees an apparatus holding a great glowing brilliance. This is the *Gigunu*, the city's crystal power source.

"There it is," Lugal shouts over the noise. Pointing to the huge ruby-red crystal, he commands, "Remove it."

The men struggle to extract the giant crystal. When they do, the power generator and all the pumping machines shut down. Amazed at the abrupt silence, they look around in sudden fear at the enormity of what they have done.

Lugal smiles.

Outside, the lights go out. The entire city of Babylon is plunged into darkness. Water flows from the dam unchecked, and the city begins to flood. A battery-powered alarm shrieks its warning into the darkness, waking the people to the emergency. They stampede in a wild rush to the temple. There they bow down to pray, begging the gods to save them. But when the unrelenting water rises up, swirling around them, they flee to the hills in terror.

———

When Eä hears about the situation in Babylon, he summons Lugal to the Abzu. Lugal obeys the command, but with deep resentment.

"What have you done?" Eä asks, demanding an explanation. "Babylon and all the surrounding cities have no water."

"The rabble support Marduk's return," he says, standing arrogant and remorseless. "They need to be punished."

Eä pauses, shocked by Lugal's attitude. "Why would you resort to such heartless action?" he asks, trying to restrain himself. "Is this how you repay your brother's trust?"

Lugal scowls at him. "I did what no one else could," he sneers. "I made Marduk leave Babylon, so what are you complaining about?"

"What you did was shameful," Eä says, growing angry at Lugal's insolent reply. "Your brother deserves better from you. Is this how you show loyalty to your family?"

Lugal seethes at the criticism. "What about you, Father? Do you show loyalty to just one son?"

Eä gasps at Lugal's impudence. A tense silence follows while he stares in astonishment. "You dare insult me, your father, and right here in our own home?" Then his fury erupts. "Go! Get out of my sight! Go where no gods ever go!"

Lugal throws him a look of hatred, and then storms out.

———

Lugal returns to Babylon with his army, determined to vent his anger. A frightened crowd gathers while Lugal's soldiers smash statues of Marduk outside the palace. Horrified, they watch as the men torch their sacred edifice. Standing in triumph, Lugal watches the flames leap from the building. He turns to instruct an officer standing nearby.

"Have them build a new temple," Lugal commands. "Then fill it with statues of *me*." With the palace blazing behind him, he leaps to a platform and addresses the crowd. "I am Lugal, god of Babylon!" he declares. "From this day forward, you will worship no other gods before me."

The people bow down to him in fear and reverence.

He beckons to a soldier. The soldier comes running. "Take a message to Inanna," he instructs. "Tell her that the time has come."

The soldier rushes away.

Observing Babylon's groveling crowd, Lugal mutters to his officer, "Nothing can stop us now." He looks back at the palace, his face illuminated by the glowing flames, and smiles with satisfaction.

———

Inanna thunders into Morgoth's city of Nippur with her army. As she passes, groups of people in the city cry out, some who fear her, others who welcome her.

"Look, Inanna!" a young woman shouts. "Inanna comes!"

"Pray to Morgoth to save us!" an old man pleads.

An older woman scolds, "Worship Inanna, you old fool. She's the greatest of gods!"

Inanna and her army race through the city. When they reach Morgoth's temple, the throng outside bows down to her.

Lugal joins her with his soldiers. "We are close to victory," Lugal says, breathless with excitement. "Hurry... let's finish it!"

Inanna summons the commander of her army, Naram-Sin. "Take your men and destroy Morgoth's temple," she orders, "while I go to Erech to dismantle Anu's authority."

Shocked by her incredible directive, Naram-Sin gazes at her in alarm. "O great Inanna, I cannot order my men to profane this holy place," he says, with a voice trembling in fear. "Morgoth will destroy us all."

Inanna looks down on him with contempt. "Have our conquests not been successful so far? I will lead you to victory, and when we finish, *you* will rule all of Sumer, not Morgoth. So have no fear of Morgoth… fear me!"

Naram-Sin watches Inanna race away from the city at the head of her army. *Did my ears hear Inanna correctly? Did she truly say that she would make me ruler of all Sumer? But what of Morgoth? Certainly, he would not simply step aside. Without any doubt, he will hound anyone to death who destroys his temple. No one dares disobey Inanna, and no one dares defy Morgoth. She tempts me with rulership, but in the end, my only reward will be death.* Confused, Naram-Sin fights down his terrible fear of both Morgoth and Inanna, one pitted against the other, but the agonizing indecision stabbing at his gut leaves him standing petrified.

When Inanna is out of sight, Lugal sees Naram-Sin standing there, gazing off into the distance like a statue. Lugal barks at him, "Well, what are you waiting for?"

Naram-Sin turns slowly and looks at Lugal with glazed eyes, as if lost in a trance.

Lugal yells more orders. "Tell your men they can carry off anything of value. Then destroy the entire temple and its foundation. Break down the enclosures of the shrine."

Instantly snapping out of his stupor, Naram-Sin barks at his soldiers. "Destroy the temple!" he commands. "Kill everyone inside! Take what you want, and then burn the city!"

Naram-Sin's soldiers instantly obey. They erect large ladders and chop their way into the temple, then slash into the crowd with swords and sabers as if mowing hay.

Seeing the carnage begin, shrieking people stampede in every direction as they try to escape the soldiers' relentless swords. Bloody victims fall right and left, screaming in agony, dropping to the temple floor, where they writhe in their final throes of death.

Lugal leaves Morgoth's city of Nippur in flames and chaos, his temple in utter ruins.

———

At Morgoth's palace at Larsa, the Council gathers to discuss Inanna's malicious alliance with Lugal. Of the original group, only five remain – Morgoth's wife, his three sons, and Varda, now the commander of the Sinai Spaceport.

"Inanna has become too dangerous," Morgoth declares. "Now that she has destroyed my city, we can no longer ignore her obvious intentions. She must be stopped."

Ninurta stands and addresses the others. "I agree. First, she laid siege to our Landing Place on Cedar Mountain, and the cities ran with blood. Then she burned the great gates of the Mountain and forced our soldiers to join her."

"She's out of control," Varda says. "She's attacking city after city, even Mission Control and the heliport stronghold at Tell Ghassul."

Nannar exchanges worried glances with Utu.

In an attempt to pacify the Council's growing anxiety, Utu speaks to them in a calm voice. "We mustn't be too hasty in our judgment," he cautions. "Perhaps Inanna just wants to punish those slaves who rebelled against her."

Ninurta turn on him with disapproval. "Don't try to protect her, Utu, just because she's our sister."

Listen to Ninurta, Utu," Varda adds. "Inanna ordered Naram-Sin to attack my command of the Spaceport at Tilmun. Even Sargon never dared cross that forbidden line, but Naram-Sin..."

Ninurta interrupts her. "Imagine that, a mortal king attacking with a mortal army!" he says, with sarcasm. Then, expressing outrage, he says, "Naram-Sin marched right through the territory forbidden to him by us. He insults us!"

Varda nods agreement. "Yes, and now he declares himself king of the Sinai," she says, incensed. "The whole area is in turmoil. With Inanna pulling his strings, I don't think he intends to stop there."

Ninurta waits for Varda's impact. Then he asks, "Can we, the rulers of Earth, tolerate such brazen insolence?"

They all pause to consider the treasonous import of Inanna's power over Naram-Sin. With her army growing stronger and more reckless every day, the old gods grows silent as the prospect of serious trouble sinks in.

"The bond between Lugal and Inanna gets stronger after every conquest," Ninurta prods. "With Lugal claiming Babylon and Inanna's attempt to seize our strategic command posts between Lebanon and the Sinai, soon they'll be impossible to stop."

The others pound the table in agreement, all but Utu who appears concerned for Inanna.

"Very well, let's put a stop to it," Morgoth says. "We can issue a decree for her trial." He gazes at Ninurta. "Then I'll send Ninurta to arrest her."

At that moment, a messenger bursts into the room, breathing hard. "Sire!" Gulping air, he says, "I bring terrible news." He bows low to Morgoth. "My Lord, your sacred temple... has been destroyed!"

The Council members gasp in unison.

Morgoth glowers at the messenger in disbelief. Angry, he waves the man away.

The messenger flinches and backs off, eager to leave.

"This time Inanna has gone too far!" Morgoth bellows.

Silence. No one dares speak. They sit gazing at Morgoth, frozen, waiting for his wrath to descend.

"Agade is doomed!" he growls, his voice rumbling with vengeance.

———

By now, Marduk knows the truth. Lugal is his bitter enemy. After Lugal's terrible deed is accomplished, Lugal abandons Babylon and goes to meet with Morgoth. His mind churning, Lugal enters the palace at Larsa.

Lugal stands before Morgoth. "I think Marduk intends to return to Babylon again," he says with caution.

"You think!" Morgoth snarls. "Anyone with a brain would be certain of it."

"I came back here to warn you," Lugal mutters, unabashed.

"Warn *me*?" Morgoth says with contempt. "After *you* destroyed his city?"

Hoping to regain Morgoth's confidence, Lugal pretends innocence. "Whatever do you mean, my Lord? I only carried out your orders."

"I never ordered you to destroy Babylon!" Morgoth roars, unable to harness his anger any longer.

"To betray your trust in me would be foolish, wouldn't it?" Lugal implores. "Destroying Babylon was the only way to keep Marduk from reclaiming his throne."

"Marduk will take revenge, mark my words," Morgoth declares. "So be warned, and warn Inanna, your accomplice."

"My accomplice? If I dared to conspire with Inanna, would I be here?" Lugal contends. "In fact, I don't even know where she is."

"Poor girl," says Utu. "Agade is in ruins. All that remains of her kingdom is a mound of dead bodies. She's so distraught that we took her back home, to recover."

Reminded of Inanna's transgressions, Morgoth smolders with anger. "She was wise to abandon her city, or I would have killed her myself for burning my temple."

Lugal gazes at him in surprise. "You're mistaken, my Lord," he says with a guileless stare. "It wasn't Inanna..."

"Not Inanna?" Morgoth asks, shocked. "Then who?" he demands, with a fierce and penetrating gaze.

"Why, I thought you knew, my Lord," Lugal replies. "It was Marduk."

"Marduk!" Morgoth says with astonishment. "Is that true?"

"I swear it," Lugal claims. "Ask Ninurta."

"My poor sister," Utu exclaims, overcome with the seeming injustice of Agade's destruction. "She had only one dream, to be Queen of the Indus, and now her beautiful palace is in ashes – for no reason!"

Suddenly stabbed with remorse for the violent action he has taken against his daughter's kingdom, Morgoth stands frozen, in a daze. His mind rolls backward...

Remembering, remembering, how he had called all Sumer's soldiers to arms. He ordered them to gather above the Indus Valley, even the savage warriors of Gutea from the Zagros Mountains. That day, a brilliant sun shone in a bright azure sky above Agade. The palace glittered below like the jewel that it was. At his command, the hordes descended on the city from all sides. They invaded the palace, killing, smashing, and stealing. When the army had finished and the city was stripped of all its beauty and value, he signaled the release of a terrible weapon. Like another sun burning above Agade, the weapon exploded, hovered, while its brilliant poison rained down on Inanna's entire kingdom. All living things died, shriveled by the searing heat. Ultimately, Inanna's lofty dreams were buried under the rubble that was once Agade.

Recovering, Morgoth stands before Lugal in a blind rage. Faced with his own folly, clawed by unrelenting guilt, Morgoth has to punish *someone*. "This time Marduk won't escape death," he snarls through clenched teeth, "no matter who tries to save him."

Chapter 10
HOLOCAUST

At Larsa, Morgoth calls an emergency meeting of the Council members. Waiting for Ninurta's arrival at the meeting, Lugal lurks in the palace corridor outside the meeting room. He knows what a risk he has taken to show up at the palace. Terrified of being recognized, he looks around with furtive glances. Suddenly, he spots Ninurta coming up the corridor.

Lugal steps out of the shadows. "Ninurta! Wait," Lugal says.

Ninurta's eyes grow wide. "You!" he exclaims. "Get out of here! Morgoth will kill you."

"I need your help," says Lugal.

"I don't doubt it," Ninurta says, frustrated by the dangerous intrusion. "But be brief," he warns. "I can't keep Morgoth waiting."

"I know," Lugal says, "but this is important." Stepping nearer to whisper, Lugal says, "When Morgoth asks you who desecrated his temple, tell him it was Marduk."

"Why should I lie for you?" Ninurta demands, growing irate.

"Because I already told him that Marduk did it."

"You know what he'd do to me," Ninurta growls, "or you, if we lie to him."

"I know," said Lugal, "but I told him you would verify it."

"Too bad for you," Ninurta snipes, pulling away. "I want no part of this."

Lugal blocks him, "Listen to me!" he commands.

Ninurta stops and stares at him. *What's going on with this little weasel?* he wonders. *Lugal sounds desperate.*

"Marduk is gathering his army right now," Lugal says. "If he is allowed to fulfill his Destiny, then *you* will never rule Earth. Is that what you want?"

"Morgoth will never let that happen," Ninurta replies, confident.

"Don't be too sure," Lugal argues, poking at Ninurta's arrogance. "If Eä defeats Morgoth, Marduk will take your crown and my kingdom," Lugal says. "We get nothing. But with Anu's weapons, we can level mountains and make the seas boil. Imagine such power!"

"You must be mad," Ninurta says in disgust. "Besides, that's treason. Anu would execute you."

"Not if Morgoth rules," Lugal argues. "But if Eä wins this war, you lose everything. Defeat him and Eä will fall, and my brother, too. Marduk is already at the Spaceport, so if you want him dead, we have to attack now."

"Attack the Spaceport? Without Anu's weapons? Impossible!" Ninurta says. "Don't bother me with such folly, unless you have the weapons." Impatient, Ninurta attempts to move away again.

Lugal grabs him. Anxiously, he looks around. No one appears to be listening. He whispers to Ninurta, "I know where they are."

———

Fearful of Marduk's growing power, the six remaining gods sit around the Council table at Larsa: Morgoth, Sud, Nannar, Utu, Ninurta, and Varda. The mood is solemn, and with the imminent threat of war, many grow anxious.

"Trouble is brewing," Morgoth warns them. "Reports tell us that Marduk's army is pressing northward from Egypt and the Abzu."

Ninurta says, "If we wait much longer, Marduk's army will be massive."

"They may even try to seize the Spaceport at Sinai," Varda adds. "If they succeed, we'd have no means of evacuating from there. Only the spaceport at Sippar remains for escape."

"He must be stopped!" Morgoth says. "The assault on my temple makes Marduk's intentions clear."

"How can anyone know that?" Utu asks.

"The fact that he was in Babylon speaks for itself," Morgoth insists.

"Marduk left Babylon for the Kur – to retrieve the symbols of power that Lugal took from him," Utu says.

Ninurta jumps to his feet. "You insult me!" he shouts at Utu.

"The truth is, Marduk was nowhere near Larsa when your temple was attacked," Utu claims.

"Are you calling me a liar?" Ninurta demands, his face red with outrage. "I swore to the Council that it was Marduk who sacked the temple."

"Let's all calm down," Nannar says. "None of us has reason to doubt you, Ninurta."

Ninurta sits down, appeased. He muses, *That was too dangerous. I hope Lugal appreciates what I am risking for him.*

Morgoth turns to Utu. "Whether you believe it or not, Utu," he says, "Marduk is the real threat to our peace."

Utu nods slightly, yielding to Morgoth's authority. *Whatever you say, Father,* he thinks to himself.

Then Utu turns to address the group. Softening his tone, he says, "Why are you all so afraid? Unless Marduk actually moves against the Sinai, we have no cause to attack him."

Morgoth considers Utu's point. "True, but we must prepare for that happening," With a rare smile, Morgoth says, "I know we are not justified in taking action unless we're certain of his intentions, Utu." Then Morgoth's voice becomes ominous. "But if Marduk does attack the Spaceport, it will mean *war.*"

———

Morgoth sent Ninurta to fly over Atlantis to see what he could find out about Eä's activities and the size of his armies. The reconnaissance was an important part of Morgoth's overall plans, and his objective was to be prepared for whatever schemes Eä might initiate.

Ninurta remembered how he had dutifully followed his father's orders. Circling above Atlantis in his Blackbird, he flew over the huge watchtower guarding the city. Below, he saw tens of thousands of Atlanteans blanketing the plane. A huge mass of sixty thousand chiefs, all with armored warriors and chariots drawn by magnificent horses, stood ready for war. So Ninurta rushed back to tell Morgoth the incredible news.

"Well?" Morgoth asked Ninurta. "What did you see?"

"Eä has a huge army," Ninurta replied, all too aware of the implications. "Thousands of Atlanteans with weapons and chariots. The entire plane outside the city was covered with them."

"So, that's how it is," Morgoth says. "I must admit, Eä has always been resourceful, if nothing else. Now that he is clearly preparing for war, we can't wait any longer. If we don't act now, he will soon be unconquerable. This is the time to strike."

"What do you want me to do?" Ninurta asked. But he already guessed what Morgoth would say.

Morgoth issued his orders. "Send the Igigi with our half-breed armies to take Athens, then Egypt. After that, we'll attack Atlantis."

If Morgoth plans to attack Atlantis, then this is my chance, Ninurta muses. *Lugal is right. We have to seize this opportunity, and we have to do it now.* He could see it all. First the Spaceport. Then Atlantis. Everything gone in a blaze of glory. It would be magnificent! All they had to do was get the weapons.

———

In Sumer, no one suspected that the world, as they knew it, was about to end. But the High Priestess Id had shown the whole disaster in Atlantis to Eä while he lay on the floor of his fortress in the Kur, his head throbbing with pain. When Bog rubbed the medallion she had given to Eä, Id came to them as an apparition, a form she used for astral travel.

Brilliant lightening flashed over the mountains west of Sumer. The explosion's immense brilliance flooded the heavens and the earth trembled to its core. A pillar of smoke rose high into the sky above the mountains. Slowly, the pillar grew into an enormous mushroom cloud, its blinding rays scorching everything in all directions. Then, driven by a furious tempest of deadly winds, the cloud began to spread from west to east. Driven by prevailing winds, the cloud roiled until it rose high as a huge mountain, a mysterious mass creeping toward the cities of Sumer.

Curious people in the cities stopped to gawk. *What can it be?* they wondered. Seeing the gigantic cloud approaching, the people began running about like chattering birds, terrified and confused. With all appearances of a dark inescapable wall descending on them, the frantic people did not know what to do or where to go.

As the storm grew in fury, propelled by a howling wind that choked the land, the evil cloud came upon the cities, enveloping them one by one. Once the plume reached the ground, it expanded slowly, creeping heartlessly toward each city, the way hot lava creeps from a volcano. The cloud pushed its way from Kish, to Nippur, then over Shuruppak, Lagash, Larsa, and even Ur. The last city to succumb to the smothering grip of the noxious vapor was Eä's city of Eridu, once the first settlement on Earth. It covered the sky and obliterated the sun, like a dark shroud, while its luminous edges cast an eerie brilliance everywhere.

————

At Varda's city of Shuruppak, Marduk rested in the Medical Center. He was still weak from the severe loss of blood he endured after the vicious wound Morgoth had inflicted. The nurses at the Medical Center marveled that he was still alive. It was a stroke of luck, they said, that Varda was there to treat Marduk when the medics brought him in from the battlefield at Larsa. Varda was known to have the ability to bring people back from the dead. Apparently, she used some remarkable medicine she called the "waters of life" and the "bread of life."

When Utu arrived at the hospital, he asked to see Marduk. The nurses told him that Marduk had been drifting in and out of consciousness, so if he wakes, Utu should not stay too long. Varda had gone already, so she would not be able to help if Marduk had a relapse. Not only that, but she had left behind only a few nurses. They were all given instructions to wait for Eä to arrive, and then they would all leave on the last spaceship for Arra. If Marduk returned to consciousness, and had gained enough strength by then, Eä could take him to safety in the mountains. Otherwise, Marduk would have to return with them to Arra for further treatment, Varda had said. Once the storm arrived, to stay in Shuruppak meant certain death.

Utu entered Marduk's room. He stared at Marduk in disbelief. Marduk lay on the bed with tubes stuck in his arms. Dark circles had formed under his eyes, and he looked pale and ghostly. Who was this person? He didn't look like the strong warrior who had led an army from Egypt to Babylon. *Great Sophia, help him recover,* Utu implored.

He went over to the bed and gently touched Marduk's hand. "Marduk," he whispered.

Marduk moaned.

"Marduk," Utu said. "Wake up! It's Utu. I must talk to you."

Marduk moaned again, his head turning toward Utu's voice as if struggling to awaken.

"Marduk," Utu said, louder this time. "Open your eyes if you can. I must know what happened at Larsa."

Marduk's eyes fluttered a bit, and then opened. He stared at Utu, as if surprised that they were both alive. "Utu," he muttered. "What are you doing here? Are we dead?"

Utu smiled at him and patted his hand. "No, we are very much alive," he said. "Eä is coming to get you."

Marduk sighed with relief. "Father is alive," he said, closing his eyes. Then his eyes grew wide, "What about Morgoth?"

Utu smiled at him. "Morgoth is dead," he said. "I watched Eä battle him from the ramparts. The war is over."

"Over," Marduk said, sighing with relief. "The last I remember was coming to tell Eä something, but then I saw a body on the floor. It was Ninurta, I think. He looked dead. Someone grabbed me from behind. Eä shouted... then a horrible pain in my side."

"That must have been Morgoth," Utu said.

"Yes, I remember now," Marduk said. "Eä and Morgoth were arguing. Eä pleaded with him to help me, but Morgoth refused. He said *his* son was already dead."

"What happened then?" Utu urged, even though he could see that Marduk's strength was fading.

"I think Eä asked about Lugal, and Morgoth said he had gone down in flames over Atlantis. He said both

172

Ninurta and Lugal were dead." Marduk closed his eyes. "I don't remember much more. An explosion, I think. Then I passed out."

Utu reached out and squeezed Marduk's hand again. "Rest now, and get well," he said.

Marduk gave him an exhausted smile. Drained, he closed his eyes and drifted back into welcome sleep.

Outside, the relentless storm moved toward Shuruppak. Utu raced to his Skybird and took off for Nippur, hoping that he could find Sud and Inanna still there. There wasn't much time left before the storm would obliterate the remaining cities. Somehow, he had to convince Inanna to leave with him, and get her to the Spaceport at Sippar before the last spaceship left for Arra.

––––––

Marduk's wife, Sarpanit, gazes out toward the distant mountains in the southwest from the balcony of her palace at Babylon. Nabu, her teenage son, joins her. He is curious about the ominous cloud creeping toward them, inching ever closer, almost like a living thing.

"Look! It's moving along the valley," Sarpanit observes, speaking as if whispering to herself."

"Great mother of all galaxies!" the boy exclaims. "I didn't believe Lugal would actually do it. How do we escape?"

"I don't know…" Sarpanit says, her voice trailing off. At once, she hurries to the telecom and punches a button, then waits for a tone to leave a message. "Eä, the evil cloud is coming, just as you said it would," she says. "If you get this message…"

Instantly, Eä's face appears on the telecom screen.

"Yes, I see it from up here in my Skybird," he says. "I'm on my way to Shuruppak now. The cloud is travelling slowly, but it will soon sweep through Babylon. Leave now, while you can. Don't pack, just go!"

"But what about the people?" she asks. "We have to help them."

"Tell them to leave," he replies, "but urge them to go only north, up into the Zagros."

"The old ones may not make it. What then?" she asks.

He pauses a moment to gather his thoughts. "If they can't escape to the mountains, they should find a cave or an underground chamber and wait there until the cloud has passed."

"What about you?" she wonders. "Will you be at Eridu?"

"No, Eridu won't be safe either," he says. "Go north like the others, and go fast. I'll find you later – with Marduk."

The screen goes dark.

Gathering courage, she turns to Nabu. "Don't be afraid," she says. "If we leave now, we can make it into the mountains before the storm reaches us."

———

Confusion arose among the older gods, for none who conspired to destroy Eä's dream had anticipated the immense cloud that descended upon them from the lands in the West. It spared no one. As the toxic wind spread death over Sumer, the great gods fled north from their beloved land.

At Ninurta's temple at Lagash, Ninurta's wife, Bau, stands outside her splendid palace overlooking the city. Together, she and her faithful eunuch watch the terrible storm approach.

"Hurry, my lady," he urges, terror written on his face. "We must go."

Bau, gazing off into the distance, appears calm. "No, I'll wait for Ninurta," she says. "Look over there," she points, "See? The storm is still far away."

"Please, my lady," he pleads. "We cannot wait any longer, or the evil wind will be upon us." He stares out at the churning cloud, torn between loyalty for Bau and the overwhelming instinct to run from certain death.

"Go then," she says, releasing him from his duty.

The eunuch runs away.

Standing alone, Bau watches the furious storm sweep into the city. As the deadly wind swirls around her, Bau cries out bitterly, "Oh Lagash, my city... my beautiful city."

Atropos cuts the thread, and the Fates must be laughing. Bau's doom is sealed.

———

Morgoth's son, Nannar, and his wife, Ningal, watch the storm advance on their palace at Ur. Nannar paces back and forth, his face clouded with worry.

Ningal gazes at him with concern. "We should leave soon," she cautions.

"Abandon our city? Never!" he explodes. "Do you expect me to just leave everyone to die?" He turns away to watch the storm coming ever closer. *How can I defend my people against something so terrible?* he wonders.

"Don't be silly, Nannar," she cajoles. "Ur was given kingship, not eternal reign. Accept that Ur's fate does not have to be your fate."

He faces her, angry but determined. "Our duty is to protect this city. Leave if you wish, but I'm staying."

She shakes her head in resignation. "Ur is my city, too," she says. *My poor Nannar,* she thinks. *Doesn't he realize that staying here means certain death?* Slowly, she picks up her needlework, sits in her favorite chair, and begins her task. "My place is here with you, so I'll stay."

By nightfall, the furies of the storm engulf the entire city. Nannar roams through the city in an effort to direct his people, but when the ill-fated wind overtakes the entire city, he faces bedlam. There is no escape. The hordes run about in blind panic.

Nannar pushes against the chafing gusts, barely able to make it back to Ningal at their ziggurat. At last, he reaches the door, and with his last strength, pushes it open. Nannar stumbles through the door, covered with gray dust.

Horrified by his deathlike appearance, Ningal runs to help him.

He collapses before her.

Distraught, with the treacherous wind rattling the door, she tries to rouse him. "Get up, Nannar," she commands. "If you stay here, you'll die." She shakes him, yelling at him over the noise of the wind, "We must get to the cellar and wait for the storm to pass."

Weak and sick, he moans. He struggles to lift himself from the floor, but he cannot.

His wife wraps an arm about him and pulls him to his feet. Supporting him, she guides him underground.

At last, reaching the safety of the cellar, Ningal helps Nannar to a couch where he can rest. She sits alone in the dim light near her feverish spouse, growing more terrified as the storm escalates. She cringes at every violent sound, fearing that the deadly storm might break through the door at any moment from outside.

"The foul smell of this wind fills me with its stench," she says aloud, as if the sound of her own voice somehow comforts her. "Listen to it!" she whispers in a hoarse voice. "Scratching at our door, howling like a hungry beast waiting to devour us."

Nannar moans in his delirious state, "Oh-h-h... Ningal." Then he calls out, "Ningal! Where are you?"

She wets a cool compress and places it on his forehead. To calm him, she strokes his head and murmurs in a gentle voice, "Hush now, my sweet one. I'm still here."

A burst of wind howls as it batters the ziggurat above. Ningal looks up, and speaking to the wind, she says, "I tremble before your power, but we will not run from you."

———

Above their cellar, the storm rolls over the city. The toxic cloud pushes into every corner of every building in its path. People run from their houses, gasping for breath. Many race wildly through the streets in search of safety. Others hide behind barriers or run to rooftops.

Choking, gasping, unable to breathe, some victims convulse with coughing while their mouths fills with foam. Others appear dazed, with pale faces and sunken eyes. They stagger about in aimless confusion, like walking dead.

Wherever these afflicted creatures wander, they soon fall to the ground, writhing, without strength to rise again. Many die a gruesome death, with mouths drenched in blood and spittle, their faces pale and ghostlike.

———

In the middle of the night, a messenger runs through the city of Erech. He shouts a warning to the sleeping populace. "Rise up! Run away, hide in the hills!"

The sleepy citizens flock outside. One person catches the messenger and stops him saying, "Wait! Why should we leave? Tell us."

The messenger stops running, and panting for air, he explains. "A deadly wind comes. Run for your lives!" The messenger tries to run on, but another citizen stops him.

"Why tell us to leave?" the citizen asks. "Inanna will protect us."

"Inanna has gone," the messenger says. "Save yourselves!" The messenger runs on.

Confused, the people look from one to another, wondering what to do. When the wind picks up, they grow anxious. Now a mob, they mill around like cattle.

An angry man shouts out, "Who caused this misery?"

Then a woman wails, "Why have the gods deserted us?"

When the storm's full fury hits, the berserk herd runs screaming through the city. Lashed by the wind, they break into buildings. Venting their rage, they smash everything inside, even the statues of their gods. As the deadly storm passes over them, they choke in their tracks, piling up in heaps. A deathly hush settles over Erech.

———

Eä took many of his frightened refugees to a place of safety high into the Zagros Mountains overlooking Sumer. From above, they all watched as the monstrous storm roared over

Sumer like a vicious beast, crushing the land and wiping out everything. No one could escape it. Cities lay in ruins, houses abandoned, roads deserted – except for the dead. Bodies lay in heaps along the roads, melting like fat in the sun. Eä watched the cloud sweep over the valley, and then into Eridu, killing every living thing left behind. Seeing the fate of his beloved city, Eä wept bitter tears.

———

Hoping to find Inanna, Utu finally reaches the palace at Nippur, a lavish residence built for Sud and her family. Fearing Morgoth's fury after Inanna's reckless attack on Larsa and Erech by her armies, she found sanctuary in Nippur.

Utu finds Inanna being comforted by their mother.

"Take care, Utu," Sud cautions, whispering to him. "She is still quite upset. The slightest reproach could send her into hysterics again."

Utu approaches Inanna, but he has no time to coddle her. "Inanna," he calls.

She looks up at him with surprise. She smiles. "Utu!" she exclaims with delight. She reaches out a hand for him. "Come, sit beside me." Then her smile fades, her body grows tense and her face, anxious. "Does Morgoth know you are here?"

"No," Utu says, hiding the truth. "I came to get you. We must leave for Arra with the others."

"Let the others go," she says, laughing. "I'm going back to my palace at Agade."

"That's impossible," Utu informs her. "The Agade you knew is nothing but rubble.

She stares at him in surprise. "But I must go back for my jewels," she says. "All my gorgeous necklaces of lapis lazuli, my diamond tiara, and all my golden rings set with emeralds, pearls, sapphires, and rubies. Do you expect me to leave my jewels and all the precious symbols of rulership given to me by Anu?"

"Forget your jewels. Those days are gone, Inanna," Utu says. "Agade has vanished into dust. You're lucky to be alive. Now the people call it *Mohenjo Daro*, the 'Mound of the Dead.' The poison infects the land everywhere, and if you return, you'll die too."

"Then I'll go to Dwarka," she says. "I can stay there until Agade can be rebuilt."

He looks at her with pity. "Dwarka is under water now, after the tidal wave that drowned Atlantis."

She stares at him with a blank expression on her face, too numbed by what he described to absorb the reality of it all.

"Do you have the Codices you took from Eä?" he asks.

"No," she replies, "Varda took them back to Arra. She said that if she gave them back to Anu, it might help save Ninurta's life."

"Ninurta is dead," Utu says.

Silence. Inanna stares again in disbelief, unable to accept the reality.

"He can't be dead," she cries. "No one is powerful enough to kill Ninurta."

"Except Morgoth," Utu states.

"No!" she cries, unable to accept the truth. "Morgoth wouldn't kill his own son."

"It was self-defense," Utu explains. "Ninurta tried to kill him – so that he could rule Earth alone."

"I don't believe you," she says, still resisting, "not unless Morgoth tells me himself."

"He can't." Utu gazes at her with a sad expression. "He's dead, too."

She grabs her head with both hands and lets out a long, ear-piercing shriek.

Sud hurries to her, but overcome with her own anguish, she is unable to ease her daughter's pain.

Utu takes Inanna in his arms, attempting to comfort her.

"You lie!" she exclaims. "Get away from me," she growls, shoving him with all her might. "Why are you tormenting me like this?" She sinks down and shakes her head. "Our father can't be dead. He just can't."

Utu grabs her by the shoulders, pulls her to her feet, and shakes her gently.

She goes limp, and sinking back down like a rag doll, she looks away with dull eyes.

"Listen to me!" he shouts into her face. "We have to leave, right now. Father is dead. Ninurta is dead. This planet is dying. We have to save ourselves."

She sits up, fully alert now, and looks into his eyes. "Who killed Morgoth?" she demands.

"I'm not sure," he says. "There was a battle, that's all I know. Marduk was wounded. I don't know who actually killed Morgoth. Maybe Eä, or his android."

"Eä, Marduk, the android? What's the difference?" she asks, never expecting an answer. "They're all from the same Arran filth. They killed everyone I ever loved!"

"None of that matters anymore, Inanna," Utu says, attempting to reason with her. "We're all responsible for this tragedy. Let's go home and forget this terrible place."

She turns on him in a rage. "Forget! How can we *forget?*" She glares at him, hatred for Eä burning in her dark eyes. "Our father's death must be avenged. I don't know how, but I'll find a way to ruin them. I'll destroy their human creatures and their beliefs. I'll never rest until I kill everyone and everything they ever cared about – no matter how long it takes."

Utu gazes at her. "Look around," he says. "Hasn't that already happened?"

"No!" she exclaims. "Not as long as Eä and his seed live."

Utu shrugs. He gazes at her with sadness, and says, "Let's go home."

———

"Poor girl," says Anu. "I keep wondering what I can do for her. She lost everything."

Id gazes at him. *Even after all the injury she caused on Earth, he still thinks of her as a little girl. How can I make him realize how dangerous she can be?* She goes to Anu and touches his arm. "Do?" she asks. "Perhaps there's nothing anyone can do. Arra may not feel like home to her now. She has no real roots here. No family of her own, no children."

"I know," he replies, "but somehow, I must keep her out of mischief."

"She still craves power," Id cautions. "I'm not sure if you could call that *mischief*."

Id did not want to argue with Anu, but his propensity to pamper and protect Inanna worried her. What could he do for a headstrong young woman with nothing else to do? Turn her loose on Arra to cause more trouble?

"The sad affairs of Earth were not entirely her fault," Anu says. He pauses to consider. "War is a dreadful thing. Inanna isn't the only one who lost family. Morgoth is gone, Antu has been exiled to Arkonia, and I am left with only remorse. I worry about the outcome of my union with Antu. I fear all our offspring, and their offspring, may be damaged – the entire line."

"Including Inanna?" she asks.

"Especially Inanna," he replies. "She thinks only of herself and her own ambitions. May the Aeons help anyone unfortunate enough to love her. Given the chance, she will glorify herself at any expense, with no concern for anyone else." Anu sighs. He looks old and weary.

"Even you?" Id asks.

Anu ignores Id's remark, as if wanting to push aside the reality. Gazing at Id, he says, "I don't trust her. If it were up to me, Inanna would never rule over others again."

Praise the Aeons, Id muses, relieved to hear that Anu has finally grasped the issue. Id waits, letting his insight sink in. Then she asks, "What about Utu?"

"Perhaps Utu has escaped Antu's curse." Anu says, then pauses to consider. "We'll have to wait and see, but until we know otherwise, Inanna will be confined to the palace. Perhaps Utu can control her, at least for now."

Id gazes at Anu with a worried frown. "I fear Inanna will go mad in captivity."

Anu shrugs. "I fear she's already gone mad."

EPILOG
WAS ANU WRONG?

Are we to believe that someone as powerful and rebellious as Inanna would simply retire to a palace on Arra, content to be a good girl after her exciting adventures as Queen of the Indus? Not likely, but did anyone describe her further exploits? Well, yes and no. One way history becomes inscrutable is by confusing us with different names for the same key players. In the case of Inanna, for example, when we look at stories about the ancient Greeks, she becomes Aphrodite; for the Romans, she is Venus. In stories of Carthage, she was worshipped as Ishtar; in India, the Hindus knew her Lakshmi. In the Celtic history of Ireland, she was the beloved Brigit.

The same was true of key dates in history. For example, historians are still arguing about traditional versus modern dates for the fall of Troy. Attempting to argue with traditional historians about the ancient past is like trying to argue with Egyptologists about the origin of the Sphinx.

According to John Anthony West, classic historians insist that we evolved in a straight line from "dumb old cave men to smart old us, with our bobble-head dolls and our striped toothpaste." History has a way of becoming legend, and some legends morph into what is accepted as truth, even though never based on historical accuracy. Facts and figures can be twisted, dates and names can be changed, just to fit the events and locations of dominant political ideologies and archaic religious practices designed to establish their "truth."

Technology now provides us with reliable methods, such as carbon dating, for probing the past in search of more credible evidence. Computer science gives us star maps that let us visualize the heavens during earlier epochs and establish accurate dates for the Giza pyramids and the Great Sphinx. Graham Hancock cites the research done by Professor Robert Schoch who showed that the Great Sphinx of Giza must have been carved at the end of the ice age, around 10,000 BC, and must be older than the orthodox date of 2500 BC set by Egyptologists. Hancock also describes the astronomical studies of Robert Bauval who first noticed how the three pyramids on the Giza plateau were in perfect alignment with Orion's belt. According to the star maps, the precise alignment actually occurred in 10,500 BC.

Hancock presents further evidence that the earth was hit by a comet between 10,800 and 9,600 BC. The resulting ice age not only plunged humanity into utter darkness, but erased any memory of the *Age of Zep Tepi*, the "first time" (36,420 BC). This was the Golden Era of advanced knowledge when the Egyptians believed that gods walked the earth. Even though the endless search for truth has produced endless arguments, the search for our true beginnings goes on. *Who are we, where did we come from, what is our true purpose?* The Age of Pisces has almost ended, the Age of Aquarius is on the horizon, and the present age of quarrels and conflict, the Kali Yuga, is expected to end in 2025. So we have something to bring us hope.

So how was Inanna's immortality interwoven with the tapestry of all these ancient events? If the writings of the great poets of history, like Homer and Virgil, are believable, then Inanna not only escaped Anu's surveillance on Arra, but she must have returned to Earth. How do we know? Because in the *Aeneid*, Virgil writes:

Are you the great Aeneas, known to fame,
Who from celestial seed your lineage claim?
The same Aeneas whom fair Venus bore
To fam'd Anchises on th' Idaean shore?

So Inanna had a son called Aeneas. His father was a prince, named Anchises. Aeneas was born on Mount Ida, about twenty miles south of Troy. Homer's *Iliad*, a Greek story, and Virgil's *Aeneid*, a Roman story, both portray Aeneas as the heroic survivor of the Trojan War. But what does the Trojan War have to do with Inanna's vendetta? To answer this question, we need to understand how the great gods of Sumer participated in the many wars that followed the destruction of the Sumerian civilization.

Troy is one of the most famous cities in history, with its story written in every language. Most people are familiar with the heroes of Troy who were glorified not only in books, but also in film – Achilles, Hector, Odysseus, Priam, and Paris. Strangely, until the ruins of Troy were found in 1822, children grew up wondering whether the Trojan War really happened or not. Even today, what actually happened in Troy more than 3,000 years ago (1194-1184 BC) seems vague and unsettling, much like the history of Atlantis or the Pyramids at Giza. Ancient traditions consider this period to be in the descending Kali Yuga (3676-976 BC), a time that Hesiod called the "Age of Heroes."

The period from 1100 to 800 BC has been called the "Greek Dark Ages." Archaeological evidence revealed great destruction to the Greek isles:

"The great Mycenaean cities and palaces collapsed. Villages and towns were burnt, destroyed, and abandoned. The population of the cities reduced drastically, there was widespread famine and people lived in isolated, small settlements. Such was the magnitude of the cataclysms that ancient Greeks entirely forgot the art of writing which they had to relearn from the Phoenicians in the 8ᵗʰ century! The ancient trade networks were disrupted and came to a grinding halt."

– Bibhu Dev Misra

Today we accept that Troy was a large and prosperous city in Anatolia (Turkey). The Trojan War was one of the most famous conflicts in history. But what made it so important, and why? Like most wars, some say it was the result of a long feud over power and wealth. In "The Trojan War" Barry Strauss wrote that the Trojans were not Greeks, but were vassals to the powerful Hittite Empire. Historians claim that Sargon the Great united all of Sumer into a single state, but the Sumerian tablets tell us Inanna urged Sargon toward that conquest.

The period from 3000 to 2316 B.C. was marked by almost constant wars. Northern Sumer became Akkad, absorbing Marduk's Babylon into Sargon's greater empire, and in time, Akkad was conquered by the Hittites and Persians. After the Trojan War, the so-called "dark ages" followed, with Greeks fighting Greeks in bloody slaughter. The battles continued during the Peloponnesian Wars (431 BC to 404 BC) and the Punic Wars with Carthage (264 BC to 146 BC), which defined the many battles that established the Roman Empire.

What role did Inanna play, and what further mischief did she provoke? After her son Aeneas was born, it is said that Inanna and her clan conspired to launch the Trojan

War. Even Wikipedia describes the Trojan War as part of Zeus's plan "to depopulate the Earth, especially of his demigod descendants." If we remove Zeus's Greek mask, and reveal him as the Sumerian Morgoth, then we see a connection to a longer history – a struggle for power over Earth that took root in Sumer. Morgoth's clan, primarily Inanna, Utu, Ishkur, Nannar, and Sud continued their vendetta against Eä, Marduk, Varda, and Eä's daughter, Geshtina.

So while Aeneas escaped the fiery destruction of Troy, historians focused on Helen of Troy, the face that launched a thousand ships. We often lose sight of Aeneas and the "other" history unfolding – the longer history of what happened *after* Aeneas escaped death at Troy. This history has far-reaching implications. The long history has less to do with Helen, the Trojan horse, or the fall of Troy, but everything to do with the influence of Inanna's manipulation of Aeneas and her desire to use him in her spiteful plan to ruin Eä's clan, and perhaps destroy the entire human race. Time compresses drastically, once we realize that all these events occurred during the 10,000 years leading up to the Kali Yuga. In fact, these events fit into one 12,600-year epoch, which is roughly half of a complete 26,000-year cycle described in the Mayan calendar.

When Troy fell, the Trojans became a people without a home. Led by Aeneas, the survivors fled from the flames of Troy. Carrying his elderly father on his shoulders, and followed by his son Ascanius and his wife Creusa, he returned to Mount Ida. In twenty ships, the Trojan survivors sailed away, only to wander the Mediterranean in search of a place to build a new Troy. Aeneas learned that Troy's rebirth was linked to his own destiny, an agenda designed and inflicted upon him by Inanna. This is his story:

Escaping the burning Troy, Aeneas sails by way of Thrace and Delos to Crete, convinced that Crete was the destination assigned to him. In a dream, he is told that Italy is his goal, so despite pestilence, he presses on to Sicily. There his beloved father dies.

When he tries to cross from Sicily to the mainland, Inanna and her mother evoke their ironclad plan for Aeneas. They raise a hurricane that blasts him to the coast of Carthage. Here, Aeneas is given sanctuary by Queen Dido, ruler of Carthage after her husband's death. She offers Aeneas stability and tranquility, and if he chooses to rule beside her, she promises him equal control of Carthage.

How could he reject a ready-made kingdom at his disposal? Aeneas explains that he would like nothing more than to stay with Dido, but accepting his destiny, he confesses to Dido that Troy's rebirth comes before his personal happiness. Heartbroken, she watches his ships leave the harbor, whereupon she falls upon a sword and dies. Servants set fire to her funeral pyre. From his departing ship, Aeneas sees the flames rise high above the city, and he realizes what Dido has done.

Although at great cost to Aeneas, once Inanna's plan was set in motion, it could not be changed. After more years of wandering and strife, Aeneas finally landed in Italy at the mouth of the Tiber River. He was welcomed by King Latinus, who later gave his daughter Lavinia in marriage to Aeneas. Did the union finally bring peace? No, the marriage provoked yet another war, and when King Latinus fell in battle, Aeneas became king. His son Ascanius (later called Iulus, or Julius), became his successor. Their descendants ruled the Romans for the next five hundred years.

So had Inanna fulfilled her curse on Eä and his human offspring, as she had vowed? Perhaps that question has not yet been answered. As the present Kali Yuga approaches its dramatic end, the outcome of our most tedious epoch will present its own evidence. At that time, the world may need no further demonstration. But even if all our questions are answered, will a new epoch begin again after our collective memory has been erased? Will the next cycle begin again, in infancy, with collective amnesia? Perhaps not, at least not for those who pursue the struggle for answers.

Many questions about humanity's past remain shrouded in mystery, drowned in the cacophony of the Mighty Wurlitzer that shouts its global messages at us from every radio and television program around the clock, messages that tell us "Lies are Truth." Until we know with certainty "Who killed JFK?", "Who downed MH-17?", "Who was behind 9/11?", and all the other nagging questions that have been buried in shredders, in rubble, and in graves, we will never find a cure for our collective amnesia. If we have forgotten who we are, it is no wonder, especially after so many who tried to tell us have been killed, or burned alive, or lost in war.

For years, the history of Atlantis has been sullied, and like Troy, its existence has been denied. Hancock states that the history of Atlantis was written on the walls of the temple at Edfu by the great god Thoth, and the story told by Plato has been verified in the translation called the Edfu texts. For many, it is a great leap of faith to accept that Atlantis may have existed at one time, let alone that there may have been survivors. Who were they? Where did they go? Some say they were the *Tuatha de Danann*, the children of Anu who landed in Ireland long ago. But if we look deeper, and remove their Irish masks, we find the *Daghda* was Enlil, and the other gods of Irish myth are his clan, including Inanna, known in Irish myth as Brigit. These were the children of Anu by Antu, a mixed race, called by some the "Dark Lords."

Did the survivors of Atlantis go north, to Scythia and the Balkans? Did they go further north, into Scandinavia, where they became the Norse gods of Wagner's Götterdämmerung, and later, worshipped by the Vikings? With their magical powers, did they become the Druids, and even later, priests in the Church of Rome, and rulers of the Vatican?

These days, we know from conventional history that Rome, the new Troy founded by Aeneas, became the seat of power in the western world. After much warfare, the western church merged with the kings and queens of the Holy Roman Empire, replacing the sacred line of Merovingian kings. As time marched on, the Cosa Nostra morphed into organized crime, and corporate technology became the military-industrial complex that provided weapons for all subsequent wars, on both sides.

While the Mighty Wurlitzer plays on, drowning out all rational thought, people wring their hands, pop their tranquilizers, and wonder, "How did the world ever get this way?" As Shakespeare's Puck said to the king, "Lord, what fools these mortals be!" Having lost the ability to think clearly, and with our amnesia kicking in with its overwhelming ability to hide the past, few of us ever ask, "Could it be that the world we see today is nothing more than the result of Inanna's determined wish for power and vengeance?"

Have the Dark Lords taken over the world? Just as in Tolkien's "Lord of the Rings," is it all about the lust for power, the insatiable desire to conquer and control all humanity? As these dark forces seem to gain more and more power, will the governments that control our lives become like "The Borg" in Gene Rodenberry's "Star Trek"? Will there be a time when all humanity will again be slaves and *resistance will be futile*? Like the proverbial snowball headed for hell, who will save us? Will Eä's son Thoth return, as he once promised, and heal the world?

———

The field of archaeoastronomy has revealed the amazing astronomical knowledge of prehistoric cultures. Graham Hancock, in "Magicians of the Gods," cites significant research concerning the origin dates of the Great Sphinx and the Great Pyramids of Giza, for example. By studying computer generated star maps, the origin dates for landmarks all over the world seem to converge on a tremendous cataclysm that marked the beginning of our present epoch – 10,800 to 9,600 BC.

Upon finding so much significant information buried in the earth for centuries past, and written in stone, hieroglyphics which we are only now able to decipher, Hancock concludes that those who left these "messages" long ago, before 9600 BC, may be trying to tell us something important. Whatever happened 11,500 years ago may repeat, *in our present time.* At that time, the Mighty Wurlitzer will cease its relentless noise, and The Matrix in which we live will crumble into dust.

Meanwhile, the *Moirai*, the three immortals who weave the intricate tapestry for all living things, still endure. They sit at the base of the Tree of Life – and they are *laughing.*

LADY LIBERTAS

As we go to press on this holiday weekend, I see pictures of the Statue of Liberty on almost every television channel, with flags waving and fireworks exploding. The whole country is celebrating the Fourth of July. Few would argue that the statue of this lady has become the most cherished symbol of our country. But how many know that her image is a replica of the Babylonian goddess Ishtar? Following in the footsteps of Lafayette, a crusader for freedom during the American and French revolutions, another Frenchman conceived and funded the idea for the statue during the American Civil War. He called her "Libertas" to honor the goddess of personal freedom worshipped by the Romans as early as the 5th century BC.

Although the doctrine of personal freedom and liberty appealed to both Greeks and Romans, even though they kept slaves, the real allure of Libertas was her principle of salvation by holy sexual relations with a temple priest or priestess. Such a union was a means of purification, and required paying the priest or priestess to confirm that it was sanctioned by the temple, and therefore "holy." According to Gregory R. Crane of the Perseus Project at Tufts University, Ishtar introduced the concept of "holy" prostitution to the human race, and over time, she became known as the "Mother of Harlots." He writes, "Harlots had been deemed social outcasts, so she was also referred to as the Mother of exiles." Since the notion of exiles relates to immigration, Libertas became the Mother of harlots, exiles, and immigrants throughout Babylonia, Assyria, Egypt, Greece, and Rome. Perhaps now we can fully understand the inscription on the base of the Statue of Liberty that welcomes immigrants to our shores.

Since Ishtar (*aka* Inanna) was such a fierce advocate of liberty, ready to take up arms and fight for freedom, she became known as the goddess of war, and because there is no freedom without victory, she was worshipped as the goddess of victory. Crane elaborates, "She was also known as the goddess of love because of her sexuality and her promotion of all types of sexual perversion in the name of freedom." Because these early people believed the goddess came from Venus and flew among the stars, they named her the Queen of Heaven.

History records the fierce warrior women who gave their lives for freedom. Note that many of these brave women have been forgotten over time, perhaps because they lacked the beauty of Ishtar that would have burned their actions into human memory. Among them are Boudicca, Queen of the Iceni tribe of Celts who dared fight the Roman army; Hypatia of Alexandria, a brilliant philosopher who was torn to pieces when she became a target of early Christian anger for teaching gnostic principles; and perhaps best known is *Jeanne d'Arc* or Joan of Arc, nicknamed "The Maid of Orléans." She became a heroine of France after she was burned alive as a witch for daring to lead her army to victory over the English.

In contrast, outrageously beautiful women who grasped and held power, even briefly, are sanctified in our collective memory. Three vivid examples come to mind. The first is Cleopatra VII, queen of ancient Egypt, who is one of the most famous female rulers in history. She is known for her exotic beauty and powers of seduction, especially her romantic liaisons and military alliances with the Roman leaders Julius Caesar and Mark Antony. Unfortunately, when she lost her grasp on power, rather than become a slave of Rome, she ended her own life.

The second example is Marilyn Monroe, goddess of the Hollywood screen. Who can forget her gorgeous body in that see-through dress she wore in "Some Like It Hot"? In less than a decade, she climbed to a pinnacle of power by bedding John F. Kennedy, then President of the United States. After her infamous "Happy Birthday" song, the ugly end came suddenly, and brutally.

The third example is the most unforgettable tragedy of all, the story of a fairytale princess who had it all and gave it up. Despite the official version, we still debate the gruesome end of Princess Diana and her lover Dodi Al-Fayed, the son of an Egyptian billionaire, on the eve of their alleged engagement. Was Diana about to find true happiness after all the misery inflicted upon her by the royal family? What would happen to her motherless boys? The story broke our hearts, and when Charles married Camilla, it simply added more insult to Diana's painful injuries.

From the beginning of human history, many women have fought the good fight. Some for power, some for freedom, some merely to survive. They remain anonymous, except in our collective memory. Perhaps because of Diana's tremendous struggle to find some form of personal liberty for herself, some have compared her face to that of Lady Liberty. If you search on Google Images, you will find the resemblance somewhat remarkable. The base of the Libertas statue has the following message:

Give me your tired, your poor,
Your huddled masses, yearning to breathe free,
The wretched refuse of your teeming shore,
Send these, the homeless, tempest tossed to me.
I lift my lamp beside the golden door.

- Emma Lazarus

Today, it somehow seems ironic that immigration might be viewed as "freedom." With the barbarians knocking at our gates, much as they did at the gates of Rome, we no longer view immigration, or homelessness, as worthy of compassion. This seems odd, since so many of our parents and grandparents arrived in America from somewhere else – homeless, tempest tossed, and yearning to breathe free.

In this epoch of the Kali Yuga, perhaps it is not so surprising to witness so many contradictions between what we claim to believe and how we actually live. Could it be that *Libertas*, as she stands so proud in New York harbor, represents the *Mystery Babylon* of Revelations? In these strange times, perhaps all strange things are possible.

V. R. R. Richards
July 4, 2016

AUTHOR BIOGRAPHY

V. R. R. Richards began as a physicist designing ballistic rockets before working on advanced computer systems in California's Silicon Valley. Later, a research program in neuropsychology led to a doctorate in human behavior, brain function, and consciousness.

After moving to northern California as a consultant, Richards focused on a lifelong ambition: developing quasi-historical science fiction stories. The tale about the ancient alien god, *Enki: Lord of Earth*, earned a place as finalist in the Pulsar Sci-Fi Contest and semi-finalist in the ASA international competition for screenplays. The second book, *Enki: Queen of Vengeance*, completes the series.

Richards now lives near the redwoods, with beloved spouse and Siamese cat.

Printed in Great Britain
by Amazon